FINNEGAN'S Promise

CAROL LYNNE

ELLORA'S CAVE
ROMANTICA®
www.ELLORASCAVE.COM

An Ellora's Cave Publication

www.ellorascave.com

Finnegan's Promise

ISBN 9781419966170
ALL RIGHTS RESERVED.
Finnegan's Promise Copyright © 2007 Carol Lynne
Edited by Helen Woodall.
Photography and cover art by Les Byerley.

Electronic book publication July 2007
Trade paperback publication 2012

FINNEGAN'S PROMISE

§

Dedication

&

Dedicated to my father, Asa Gillette, who passed away from lung cancer in May 2005.

Chapter One

ဢ

Calder Finnegan entered the smoky pub and looked around. It never changes, he thought. He'd been away from the bar for almost six years. His eyes roamed the crowd of people drinking and laughing. Some of the faces had changed in the small Irish pub but the atmosphere was essentially the same. It was a long room with about fifteen tables and ten booths all lined up like little soldiers. The small stage, used for traditional Irish music looked like it was in need of some repairs. Fin wondered if his da would mind if he made a few upgrades here and there while he was here.

The only thing that was still perfect about the pub was the long mahogany bar. Oh and the delicious bartender standing behind it. *Yum, who was he?* Da sure didn't employ anyone who looked that good last time he came in. Fin decided to take a seat in the back corner of the pub and get the lay of the land.

The bar was packed with twenty- and thirty-something customers. When he was growing up it seemed the bar was frequented by dock workers and other blue-collar types, most fairly old. Back then, the pub's heaviest traffic came right after five o'clock when the workers got off. They'd stop off at Finnegan's for a beer or two before going home to their families. Occasionally, men would bring their wives and girlfriends to the pub on a Friday or Saturday night to listen to music, but that was it. This crowd was completely different from what he was used to.

Now Finnegan's held a broad spectrum of patrons. Everyone from college kids to guys in suits. Fin shook his head. What the hell was going on in the small lazy pub his da had chosen over him and his mom? Fin felt the anger returning at the thought of his mom. He pushed the thoughts away and concentrated on the bartender. God, he was amazing. He stood maybe six feet tall, with the dark black hair and brilliant blue eyes of the black Irish. His body was lean but not skinny, muscles corded in ropes on his arms and neck. Fin wondered what his chest looked like. Damn, now he was getting hard. This was definitely not the place for him to lust after a man. It could totally ruin his career if anyone saw him staring at Mr. Gorgeous with a stiff cock in his jeans.

To help hide his identity, Fin wore a baseball cap with his shoulder-length black curly hair tucked up inside.

He continued to watch the bartender entertain the crowd. He told jokes and laughed at the stories and people surrounding him. He seemed to be the main attraction in the pub. Fin watched him do a few tricks with the liquor bottles while filling drink orders. He was absolutely amazing.

The small band of musicians started up again but Fin's eyes remained on the bartender. God, he could so not do what he wanted to. He would be the laughingstock of professional football if anyone found out he preferred the players to the cheerleaders. Fin looked around to make sure no one was watching and thumped his rampant cock. He had to get himself under control. He looked toward the bar and noticed a brilliant set of blue eyes looking right at him. Fin's mouth went dry and his palms started to sweat. He quickly averted his eyes to the musicians on the stage. When he looked back the hunk behind the bar was busy doing another one of his bottle tricks.

The customers began to chant. "Mick…Mick…Mick…Mick."

Fin looked around. Who the hell was Mick? He watched the bartender jump up on the bar and take a bow. So that's what Mr. Gorgeous' name was.

"Sing for us, Mick!" someone in the crowd shouted. The rest of the patrons chimed in, clapping and whistling. He gave the people a beautiful dimpled smile then turned and looked right at Fin. His eyes felt like a caress on Fin's skin. Mick jumped off the bar and headed for the stage.

He spoke quietly to the musicians and began singing the Irish ballad, "The Banks of Lee". Fin's jaw dropped in awe. The man had a voice that would make any Irish tenor jealous. The notes were so perfect they touched his soul.

He caught Mick's eyes seeking him out at several points during the ballad. Mick finished the song and did a quick bow before jumping back over the bar to resume his duties. The crowd was still cheering as Mick went back to mixing drinks.

With his cock finally under control Fin approached the bar. He leaned on the end watching Mick, waiting for his turn. Finally, Mick turned and Fin was captured.

He walked over to Fin and wiped the bar in front of him with a rag. "What can I get for you, friend?"

Fin didn't dare say what he was thinking. "Build me a Guinness please." Mick nodded his head slowly and smiled. Fin almost groaned. He wanted to stick his tongue in those perfect dimples. Mick looked older close-up. Fin guessed him to be around thirty.

"One Guinness coming up." Mick turned to slowly but expertly build Fin a Guinness. They referred to it as building a Guinness because the added nitrogen caused the Guinness to foam so much that a good bartender took his time while drawing the dark beer from the tap, adding layer upon layer until the glass was full with just the right amount of foam. When he was done he handed the drink to Fin. "Not many people ask for that anymore. The customers today all want Mexican beer." Mick shook his head. "Why they come into an Irish pub for Mexican beer is beyond me." He wiped the bar down again and smiled.

Fin dug his wallet out of his pants and put a ten on the bar. "They come in for you. You're the best bartender I've ever seen. The best singer too." When Mick tried to hand him back his change Fin held up his hand. "No. Keep the change."

He held out his hand to Mick. "I'm Calder Finnegan. My da probably told you he asked me to come to Boston during the off-season so he could take this trip back to Ireland."

Mick's eyes seemed to lose some of their shine. He rubbed his wet hands on his faded jeans and shook Fin's hand. "Nice to finally meet you, Calder. I'm Dominic 'Mick' Sullivan."

"I'll let you get back to your customers. I'm going to drink this and head to Da's, but I'll be back before opening tomorrow…and please call me Fin." At Mick's nod Fin went back to his table and drank his Guinness. When he finished he waved to Mick as he left.

* * * * *

Mick stared after Fin. "Damn." He shook his head. How he'd not recognized the football star was beyond him. How was he going to work alongside Calder Finnegan, knowing he could never touch the all-star running back? Sean hadn't told him Fin was going to take up the slack when he went to Ireland. He needed to call Sean before his plane left in the morning. Mick looked at the clock. Eleven-thirty. Mick wondered if Sean would still be packing.

He picked up the bar phone and dialed Sean's number while still filling drink orders. Sean picked up on the third ring.

"Hello?"

"Hi, Sean, it's Mick. I hope I didn't wake you." Mick handed a waitress the last of her drink order. "I just met Fin. He stopped by on his way to your house. Why didn't you tell me he's going to help out while you're gone?"

"I didn't tell you because I wasn't sure he'd really come. As you know we've not had the best relationship since his mom died. I called him a month ago. I guess it took him until the last minute to make up his mind, but I'm glad he did. Otherwise you'd be working thirteen-hour days for the next month."

Mick sighed. He knew Sean was right, he would need the help. He just wasn't sure if Fin was the kind of help he needed. "When he gets there tell him I'm sorry I didn't recognize him. Say I'll meet him downstairs at ten tomorrow morning." Mick filled more drink orders and made change. "What time does your flight leave, Sean?"

"Eight in the morning and if Fin is here there won't be a need for you to take me." Sean seemed to think for a minute. "Mick? Please don't tell Fin about the cancer. I'll find a way to tell him when I get back."

Mick stopped what he was doing and ran his hands through his short black hair. "I don't understand why you haven't told him, Sean. You've known for two months. Why are you gonna waste a month in Ireland when you could be spending it with Fin?"

"That's my business, not yours. I'm doing all of this for a reason and it's not just running away like you seem to think. The doctors say I've got six months left before I start really getting sick and there are a few things I need to accomplish before I go. Now can we just leave it at that for a while?"

Mick swallowed around the lump in his throat. He loved Sean like the father he never had. "Okay. I'll trust you on this. You don't have to worry. I won't tell Fin anything while you're gone."

"Thanks Mick. I'll see you in a month. Is there anything I can bring back for you?"

"Just you, old man. Just make sure you come back."

"Bye, Mick. Take care of Fin. He doesn't seem to be a very happy man despite his fame and fortune."

"Bye. Have a good trip."

Mick hung up the phone and had to step around the corner of the bar to dry his eyes. He didn't understand what Sean was thinking but Sean always seemed to have a plan. Mick would have to trust that he really knew what he was doing this time around.

* * * * *

Fin knocked on the front door of the brownstone he'd grown up in. He'd only been back to Boston a couple of times since his mom's death six years ago, and he wasn't at all sure he could live in this house for the next month. The front door opened and Fin hardly recognized the older man standing in front of him. His da had aged a lot in the last few years. "Hi, Da."

Sean Finnegan pulled his only child into a warm embrace. "I'm so glad you decided to come home, Calder." Sean stepped back into the hallway and let Fin enter the house. Carrying a large suitcase, Fin walked into the living room followed by Sean.

Fin looked around the living room. "Everything looks exactly the same." Fin turned toward his da with a question in his eyes. "Why does everything look exactly the same, Da? It hasn't changed at all since the day Mom died. Not even the crochet basket beside her chair."

Sean looked around the room like he was seeing it for the first time in a long time. He shrugged his shoulders and sat in his chair. "Why would I? Your mom worked hard to make this house a home."

Fin swallowed and looked away. "I don't want to argue with you tonight, Da." Fin sat on the blue floral sofa to his da's right. "I stopped by the pub tonight on my way over. It was kind of weird. The pub is so different yet everything is the same. Same tables and booths, same décor, same bar, everything looks just like it always has except the customers. When did Finnegan's become a hot spot for the college kids and young professionals of Boston?"

Sean smiled. He was very proud of his pub, always had been. "It started changing the day I hired Mick Sullivan. He's got the kind of personality people flock to. I sold him the apartment above the bar three years ago."

Fin was shocked. "You sold him the apartment? I thought that run-down place was a rental only. How could you sell the top floor of the building?"

Sean smiled and shrugged again. "It's the only way he'd live there. I was getting too old to do the maintenance required on it and I got tired of people skipping out still owing me rent. So I talked to Mick about it and he said he'd buy it as long as I'd also sell him ten percent of the pub." At Fin's shocked face, Sean continued. "He doesn't seem to care anything about making decisions for the pub or the profit that's earned from it. What he was after was job security for as long as he lived there. So...tell me what you thought of him?" Sean gestured to the baseball cap still on Fin's head. "Nice hat, by the way."

Fin reached up and took the cap off. His black curls fell to his shoulders. "Sorry about that. I put it on to go into the pub. I wanted to check things out without anyone recognizing me." He set the cap beside him on the sofa. "Mick seemed like a...nice enough guy. I didn't get a chance to talk to him long but he builds a good Guinness."

Sean nodded his head. "Yeah, the man sure does know his business. He called before you got here, by the way. Wanted to let me know you were coming. He told me to apologize for not recognizing you. It seems your hat had the desired effect. Mick said to meet him in the pub at ten tomorrow morning." Sean brushed imaginary lint off his pants. "I was hoping you could take me to the airport too. My flight leaves at eight but I should get there around six-thirty."

"Sure, I'll take you, Da. Is your cousin Peter meetin' ya at Shannon Airport?"

"Yeah. I left his number beside the phone in case you need to get a hold of me for something. We won't be there the whole time, we plan on doing some traveling around the country, but we'll at least call and check messages."

Fin yawned. "Sorry, I'm going to have to get to bed if I'm going to be up and dressed by six to take you to the airport." Fin stood and started up the stairs, carrying his bag.

Sean called to him as he got to his bedroom door. "It's good to have you home, son."

Chapter Two

ဢာ

Fin dropped his da at the airport and drove back to the house. He wandered around the old place, lost in his memories. He could still picture his mom crocheting in front of the TV, waiting for his da to come home. Evelyn Finnegan waited for his da a lot. Sean had always put the pub first on his list of priorities. Fin didn't think his da had ever seen one of his football games. His mom had though. She was always in the front row cheering him on.

Evelyn was the kind of mom every child dreamt of. All the kids in the neighborhood opted to play at Fin's house because his mom would make a fresh batch of cookies for them. She was the one who soothed his scrapes and held him when he was sick. It wasn't that his da was ever mean to him or his mom, he simply was never around. Fin grew up seeing his da for about ten minutes a day. Sean would make it a point to join his family for breakfast before Fin headed off to school but that was it. His da had Sunday evenings off because the pub closed early but he always stayed late to work on the accounts. He did see his da at the supper table on Monday evenings but that was only because the pub was closed.

Fin shook his head. He had to get out of this melancholy mood. He decided to go for a run before meeting up with Mick. Fin raced upstairs to change into his workout clothes and took off down the street. As he ran his normal ten miles his mood lightened. After a quick shower and a change of clothes, he headed for the pub, feeling much better.

* * * * *

15

Mick was restocking the bar when Fin came in. Mick looked different this morning. He was wearing small wire-framed glasses. Fin liked the look on him. As a matter of fact, Fin liked everything about the look of him.

Mick finished filling the beer cooler and stood up to shake Fin's hand. "Good morning. I thought I'd get a head start on the day." Mick smiled and shrugged. "I couldn't sleep so I've been down here awhile." Mick poured himself some fresh coffee and set it on the bar. "Could I interest you in a cup of coffee this morning?"

"I'd love a cup, thanks." When Mick turned to get another cup off the shelf, Fin couldn't help but notice Mick's tightly muscled ass in the softest-looking jeans he'd ever seen. He was lost in the sight when he finally realized what he was doing. He jerked his head up and saw Mick watching him in the mirror behind the bar. Fin averted his eyes. He could feel a blush slowly working its way to his ears.

Mick turned around and placed the coffee on the bar. "So…how're we going to work out our schedules while Sean's in Ireland?" He came around the bar and sat on the stool right next to Fin.

Fin tried not to let the close proximity of Mick's thighs bother him. "Why don't you tell me what you and Da have already worked out and I can just follow his schedule." Mick took a drink of his coffee and licked his lips. Fin almost moaned at the sight.

"Usually Sean opens the pub and I come down to work around three or four. Jeff, the cook, only works the lunch and early evening crowd. He leaves around seven o'clock so no food is served after that except your normal bar munchies for the night crowd. We have three waitresses who work in two shifts. Sally should be here anytime and then she leaves at seven o'clock as well. She's got a family she needs to be with in the evening. Then there's Lisa and Mel. They get here about six o'clock and work until we close at two."

Fin nodded his head. "Okay. So what hours does Da usually work?"

Mick looked confused. "What do you mean? Sean's usually here from the time the pub opens until we close down for the night."

Now it was Fin's turn to look confused. "He's still working sixteen-hour days at the age of sixty? Why?"

Mick put his hand on Fin's shoulder and squeezed slightly. "He's got nothing left to go home to, Fin."

Fin didn't know whether to be angry with his da or feel sorry for him. He quickly decided on anger. "Well, he wasn't any different when he did have something to go home to. This pub has always been his true family." Fin got up and paced around the bar, trying to find something to take his mind off his da.

He could feel Mick's eyes on him. Finally, Mick cleared his throat and pushed away from the bar. "I think you should see something. Follow me."

Fin followed Mick down the hall and into his da's office. He stepped through the doorway and stopped. The walls were covered with pictures. There were action shots of him during various games, publicity pictures and magazine covers. All framed behind glass. Fin turned to look at Mick. He pointed toward the pictures on the wall. "When did Da put all this up?"

Mick looked at him and shrugged. "I don't know. The walls have been full of your pictures since I've known Sean."

Fin stared at the walls. He felt like his chest was going to implode any minute. He felt the sting of his eyes and knew he was about to cry. He quickly excused himself and went into the restroom.

Fin ran to the sink and turned the cold water on. Taking deep breaths, he splashed the cool water over his face. "Why, Da? After all these years…why are you proud of me now?" Fin turned the water off and leaned against the wall. He slid down until he sat with his face buried in his hands. His knees rose to support his arms. He wasn't crying. He just couldn't seem to get enough air into his lungs. Fin heard the door open and felt a warm body slide down beside him.

Fin knew it was Mick but he didn't look at him. Mick didn't say anything, he just sat with him. After a while Mick finally spoke.

"He's very proud of you, Fin. From what I hear from the old-timers he always has been." Mick reached a hand out and rubbed circles on Fin's thigh.

Fin closed his eyes. He was trapped between thoughts of his da and the warm caressing hand of the man sitting next to him. Fin realized that Mick's soothing must have helped because he began to feel better. He turned his head and rested it on his arm, looking at Mick. "Thank you for telling me and for…well, you know."

Mick raised his hand off Fin's thigh and stroked the top of his head. "You're lucky, you know? My dad didn't even love me enough to stick around after my fourth birthday." Mick looked at him and leaned a little closer. "Sean might not have always shown you but I do know that man loves you something fierce."

Fin looked into Mick's eyes and then looked away again. "Well…I guess we'd better get going. The pub should be opening any time and I need to still meet Jeff and Sally." Fin got up and put his hand out toward Mick.

Mick looked into Fin's dark green eyes and let him pull him up. They stood there looking at each other for several moments. Finally Mick let out the breath he'd been holding. "Let's get to work."

* * * * *

It was almost eleven o'clock and Fin felt worn out. He'd helped Mick behind the bar and helped the waitresses as much as possible over the past week and a half. One thing he could do was take over the deep fryer. Most of the nighttime munchies were prepared by the waitresses. Nothing fancy, just pub fries, nachos and cheese-stuffed jalapeño peppers.

Fin watched Mick with increasing interest. He could swear that Mick had come on to him a couple times over the last ten days. It wasn't anything obvious, just looks that lasted too long or touches that felt more intimate than friendly. Fin shook his head. He didn't know what they meant but he did know his cock had been hard for the last few hours. He even caught Mick looking at it a couple times. Maybe, just maybe, this month would go better than he thought.

"Hey, Fin. Wake up!" Mick called to him. "I need you to get me another keg of Sam Adams, if you would please."

Fin gave him a quick nod and headed to the basement where they kept the cooler that held the big kegs. He was thankful for his strength as he hefted the keg over his head and wove through the growing crowd of people. He lowered the keg once he was behind the bar and knelt down to change the hoses from the empty keg to the new one. Fin was so busy changing the keg he didn't even notice when Mick came to stand right beside where he knelt. He finished with the keg and turned his head to find Mick's cock right in his face. Mick's erection was clearly outlined by the soft faded denim of his jeans. Fin swallowed, trying to ease the lump that formed in his throat and stood up.

Mick shifted at the last minute to reach across the bar to put some drinks on Mel's tray. Fin swallowed again and stood just behind Mick. Mick deposited the drinks on the tray and straightened again. He looked over his shoulder at Fin and subtly stepped back into Fin's rock-hard cock. He slowly moved his ass from side to side, rubbing himself against Fin's erection.

Then he just walked away as if nothing had happened. Leaving Fin to face the crowded bar with the biggest hard-on of his life. Fin stepped closer to the bar to hide the bulge in the front of his jeans. Luckily for him Lisa stepped up to the bar with a food order.

Fin took the order and headed toward the kitchen. He got the frozen cheese-stuffed jalapeño peppers out of the freezer and put them in the deep fryer. While he waited for the peppers he assembled two plates of nachos and slipped them into the microwave. He was about to turn around when he felt a warmth against his back and a hard cock against his ass. Two arms came around him and pulled him back even farther against the man behind him.

Mick licked Fin's neck and Fin moaned. "Stay with me tonight." He continued to rub his erection against Fin's ass until the deep fryer beeped, letting him know it was time to take the peppers out.

Fin turned in Mick's arms to face him and licked his lips. "I guess after the evening of teasing you've handed me I'm not going to have much choice." Fin looked down at his cock. It looked like it was trying to break through the zipper on his jeans.

Mick quickly ran a hand down its length and cupped him. "Save this for me, will ya?" He turned and went back into the bar. As soon as he crossed the threshold the crowd began to yell for another song.

Fin quickly finished the munchies and headed back into the bar. He didn't want to miss a single note of Mick's song. Mick stood on the stage, talking softly to the musicians. He seemed completely oblivious to the erection still evident in his jeans. Maybe that's why all the women crowded around the front of the stage. The song he sang tonight was a little livelier than his normal ballads but just as beautiful.

* * * * *

The two of them covertly flirted with each other the rest of the night. Finally the customers left and they began cleaning up the pub. After everything was cleaned and put away for the night Lisa and Mel left. Mick locked the door behind them and turned toward a waiting Fin.

He walked toward Fin with hooded eyes. When they were standing toe to toe, Mick cupped Fin's cheek. "As hot as I am for you, I don't want a quick fuck up against the bar. I want to take you upstairs to my king-sized bed and lick every inch of that beautiful body of yours." He brushed a whisper of a kiss across Fin's lips and held out his hand in invitation.

As they climbed the stairs Fin started to have second thoughts. What if someone found out about this? He wasn't sure it was worth the risk until he glanced up and his face was a few inches from Mick's fine ass. Okay, maybe it was worth it. He hadn't had sex since he'd been in the pros and before that, it had only been in dark back rooms of the gay clubs he'd frequented in college. It was just too easy to have sex with someone and then have them turn around and sell their story to the tabloids. Fin thought Mick was different though—at least he hoped he was.

At the top of the stairs Fin couldn't believe his eyes. The dingy old apartment had been transformed. "Wow. This is absolutely beautiful. I mean…I can't believe this is even the same place."

The whole loft had been gutted and opened up. Everything had been redone in the Craftsman style with heavy woodwork. The main room consisted of a living room-kitchen combination. The rooms were separated by a built-in beautifully crafted breakfast bar. The furnishings were simple but created a homey feel despite the soaring ceiling.

"Thanks. It took a lot of work but it was worth it. I was lucky enough to find a damn good carpenter to do everything I couldn't do myself. I've still got a few things to do. I'd like to replace all the windows." Mick looked away from the room and back to Fin. "I'm going to get a beer. Would you like one?"

"Yeah, I would. I hope you don't mind me asking but could I take a quick shower while you're getting them? I kinda smell like French fry boy."

Mick laughed and headed toward the kitchen. "Sure thing. The bathroom's through that door and to your right. I'll lay out something for you to put on after you're done."

Fin headed toward the bathroom. It was tough but he resisted the urge to stroke himself off. After toweling dry he noticed the pajama bottoms lying on the bed. He quickly put them on and went back to the living room. Mick was sitting on the couch. He'd also changed into lounge pants, only his were made of white satin. Fin didn't see any reason for pretense so he sat down on the couch right next to Mick.

Reaching over, Mick, traced his jaw with his fingertips. "You're so gorgeous."

Fin felt his cheeks flush, but said nothing as Mick continued to map Fin's face with his fingers. Mick slid his hand down Fin's neck to brush over his chest.

Mick groaned as Fin's nipples pebbled under his soft touch. Looking from his chest to his eyes, Mick smiled. "I like a man who's responsive." He left Fin's nipples and traveled down to the six-pack abdomen Fin had worked so hard to maintain.

Mick moaned as his touch set the muscles in motion.

Fin felt his cock grow harder by the second as Mick neared the waistband of his pajama bottoms. Instead of continuing however, Mick worked his way back up to Fin's nipples. He tweaked one with his fingers as his mouth closed over the other.

Fin felt the flick of Mick's tongue as he suckled. He thought he'd go mad before Mick finally pulled off and kissed his way up Fin's neck.

With a soft swipe of his tongue across Fin's closed lips, Mick urged Fin to open.

Sighing, Fin opened his mouth and let Mick's tongue slide in.

It was like setting a match to dynamite.

Mick opened wider and his own tongue found its way into Fin's mouth. Fin needed to be closer to the man in his arms. He repositioned him so that Mick was sitting on his lap straddling his thighs. He thrust his cock against Mick's satin-covered erection. "God, you feel good. It's been way too long though. I probably won't last."

Mick ran his fingers through the long curls of Fin's hair. He slid his ass back and forth across Fin's cock. Fin couldn't help but notice the way Mick's cock was dripping pre-cum all over the white satin pants, making them transparent. Mick moved from Fin's lips to his neck licking and sucking his way down to the hollow of his throat. He swirled his tongue into the little indentation and began caressing Fin's chest.

Fin rested his head on the back of the couch and let Mick taste him. He continued to thrust up against Mick's ass. When Mick moved to suckle and bite his nipples Fin knew he couldn't last much longer. He reached down and pulled Mick's very impressive cock out of his pants and began stroking him in time with his own thrusts against Mick's ass. Fin reached his other hand inside Mick's pants and ran his fingers down Mick's crevice. That's all it took for Mick to come. Mick's body vibrated so hard on Fin's lap that his own cock gave up the fight and erupted inside his pajama bottoms. Mick collapsed against Fin's chest and Fin wrapped his arms around him.

They were both breathing so heavily neither of them could say anything. Finally Mick raised his head and looked at Fin. "Wow, that was something else."

Fin smiled and raised his head to steal a kiss. "Mmmm…it was…but now I'm gonna need another shower." He smiled and thrust his wet pants against Mick's ass.

Mick nodded and stood up, his cock and nut sac still hung out of his satin pants. He looked down at himself and smiled. "Let's both take a shower and go to bed." He pulled Fin up and led him toward the shower.

Mick stripped and put clean towels out before turning on the shower. Fin watched him move around the bathroom while he undressed. The sight of Mick's cock was too much temptation and he sank to his knees in front of him. Mick had a beautiful cock. It was large for a man as lean as he was. Fin traced the veins down from head to root. He cupped Mick's sac and gently squeezed. "God, I want to taste you so badly it's killing me."

Mick thrust his now-erect cock toward Fin's mouth. "Be my guest, I'm clean. I've got the paperwork in the other room and I haven't been with anyone for over a year."

Fin looked up at him sheepishly. "I'm clean too. I haven't been with anyone since I turned pro." Fin shrugged before taking Mick's heavy cock deep into his mouth. God, he'd missed this. Fin loved sucking cock. The feel of the soft skin over hard muscle on his tongue drove him crazy. Fin swirled his tongue around the head a few times and then dipped his tongue into the slit at the top. Mick tasted fantastic. There was absolutely no bitterness to his essence. Fin opened his throat and took Mick's cock all the way down to the base.

Mick jerked and thrust his hips toward Fin's face. "Fuck, that feels good. Oh God… Fin, you'd better stop before I come. I still plan on fucking your hard ass." Mick pulled Fin to his feet and leaned in for a taste of himself on Fin's tongue. "Damn, baby, you're good at that. Why haven't you had sex in over seven years? With a mouth like that it should be a crime."

Fin continued kissing Mick as they entered the shower. The shower was perfect for fucking. It was big and sturdy with a bench built into one corner and a chest-level ledge running around one side.

Fin broke the kiss to look into Mick's beautiful blue eyes. "I've never trusted anyone not to out me to the press before you. I've had a few reporters bring up the fact that I've never been seen with a woman, but I just let it be known that I didn't have time for a personal life. This is the time to concentrate on my career and a personal life would have to wait." He shrugged. "They seemed to have bought it because no one's brought it up in a while."

Mick seemed startled by that comment. He pulled back and looked into his grass-green eyes. "Why do you trust me so much after only knowing me for ten days?"

Fin leaned forward and licked water spray off Mick's neck. "Because my da trusts you. If I know nothing else about my da at least I do know he's a good judge of character." Fin ran his hands down Mick's back to his ass and squeezed. "I love this ass."

Mick shifted his hands to Fin's cock. "I can't decide whether I'd like to fuck you or be fucked by you." He continued to stroke Fin's cock with both hands.

Fin licked Mick's lips. "Fuck me, Mick."

Mick turned Fin around and put his hands on the ledge. "Hold on to the ledge, baby. I'm going to have to use some shower gel. I'll get some lube tomorrow." Fin rested his head on his outstretched arm while Mick squirted gel into his hand.

Fin moaned and thrust toward his fingers as he added one finger and then slowly a second finger. "Feels fucking amazing. Keep going." He thrust back again as Mick substituted his cock for his fingers. Fin impaled himself slowly on the full length of Mick's cock. "Oh God, it burns so good. Fuck me hard, Mick."

Fin held on to the ledge as Mick pounded the full length of his cock in and out of Fin's ass. Mick thrust into him so hard he knew one or both of them would be bruised by morning. Mick leaned forward a little and bit Fin's shoulder blade as his cum exploded deep into Fin's ass.

Before Fin had a chance to come Mick spun him around and swallowed his cock. Fin thrust his cock down Mick's open throat four times before he came with a shout that rattled the windows.

After catching their breath they got out and dried each other off. Still touching him, Mick led Fin to his bedroom. The room was decorated in shades of green with white accents. He went to the bed and pulled down the sage green comforter. He kissed Fin. "Get in bed, baby. I've gotta make sure everything is locked up tight for the night. I'll be right back."

Fin slipped into bed and was in heaven. Mick had white satin sheets that felt cool on his skin. It made the unseasonably hot May temperature outside bearable. Fin stretched out and folded his hands behind his head. He couldn't believe the turn his life had made in the last twenty-four hours. The sex in the shower had been the best of his life. Well worth waiting seven years for. Fin hoped Mick would want to continue this budding relationship between them but his lack of self-esteem was starting to put doubts in his mind.

Mick came back to bed, turning lights off as he went. He crawled in beside Fin and snuggled right into his chest. "There was a message on the answering machine from Sean. He has finally called to say he'd made it to Ireland all right. He said he'd call again next Sunday night to check in." Mick rubbed his five o'clock shadow over Fin's chest. "Thank you for trusting me, Fin."

Fin reached down and pulled him up for a kiss. "Don't thank me. I was just thinking the sex we just had in the shower was the best of my life. I should be thanking you." Yeah, his nerves were definitely getting the better of him. He cleared his throat and rubbed Mick's back. "Do…do you think we could do this again sometime?"

Mick stilled in his arms. "I don't know what you think of me, Fin, but I don't have casual sex with just anyone. You said you trusted me? Well, I trusted you too. I trusted that this was more than a casual once in a while kind of arrangement. I'd like to continue seeing you every night until you get sick of me or have to leave…whichever comes first."

Fin kissed him. He put more feeling into the kiss than he'd allowed himself before. "I didn't mean to offend you. I know everyone looks at my size and my position and thinks I'm just another conceited jock but that couldn't be further from the truth." Mick snuggled in against his neck to listen and Fin ran his hand over Mick's short black hair. "I've always been very self-conscious. I don't know if it's all the mixed-up feelings between Da and me or what. I've just never felt I was good enough. Football's the only thing I've ever excelled at. Hell, even my college degree is a joke." He took a deep breath and released it slowly. "I guess it's just hard for me to believe I'm good enough for someone besides my mother to care about. You might have to bear with me while I try to work it out with myself."

Mick kissed his neck. "I already care about you. Believe me when I tell you that if my feelings change toward you you'll be the first to know. I don't like games of that nature. More than anything though, I don't want to fall in love with you."

Fin tensed in Mick's arms. Why should Mick be any different from anyone else? he thought.

Mick kissed his neck again. "I don't wanna fall in love with someone I know is going to leave. I also don't wanna fall in love with someone who's still so far in the closet that I can't take him dancing or out to dinner like a real couple."

Fin resumed petting Mick's hair. "I understand what you're saying. I feel the same way about being afraid of love. I wish I had the kind of career where it wouldn't matter if I was gay or not but unfortunately I don't. The professional football league is still most definitely not a good career choice for an openly gay man. I've still got a few more good years left in me to play. It sucks but I guess I'll have to put the rest of my life on hold until I retire." Fin rubbed his hand over his eyes. "Every day I wake up I feel like a fraud and a liar. I don't have a single friend in New York because I'm paranoid I'll let something slip. During the season I spend my days either working out or at practice and my nights parked in front of the

TV usually. I just wish I could be what I am and still play the sport I love."

After Fin finished Mick climbed on top of him. He straddled Fin's thighs and started stroking his cock. "You've got a friend now. For as long as ya want me. I won't like it and I can't promise we won't fight over you being buried in the closet but I'll never out you." He leaned down and gave Fin a passionate series of kisses. "Would you make love to me once before we go to sleep? I don't have any lube but I've got hand lotion on the table beside the bed."

Fin smiled and flipped Mick so he was under him. Fin reached for the lotion and squirted a good dollop on his hand. He slid down Mick's body until his face was even with his spread ass cheeks. "Spread 'em wider for me. I want to taste you first."

Mick groaned and hooked his knees over his arms, presenting his hole. "Yeah, baby. Taste me."

Fin rimmed the puckered hole with his tongue. Sucking and licking, he slowly pushed his tongue into Mick's hole. Mick groaned and tightened the muscles of his ass on Fin's tongue. "Please, Fin, I need you in me." Mick panted as Fin watched the muscles in his stomach ripple. Licking his way back up Mick's crevice, Fin mouthed his sac as Mick continued to moan. Fin smiled to himself, he'd never gotten anyone so worked up before. He decided to play a little more by nipping at the tender skin around Mick's cock.

"Oh God... Oh baby... Please..."

When he thought Mick had been teased enough, Fin took the hand with the lotion and prepared Mick's hole. He sat up on his knees, lubed his cock and put Mick's legs over his shoulders so he could get as close as possible. He lined up his cock and pushed in very slowly, drawing out Mick's pleasure. Mick took all of him and screamed for more. Fin started pumping his cock in and out of Mick, slowly building up speed and pressure as he went. The harder he thrust, the more Mick seemed to love it. Mick ended up with his knees over his own head, almost touching the mattress as Fin pounded in him as hard as he could. "Oh Mick...oh gonna come, sweetheart."

Mick started stroking himself hard. "Come inside me, baby." Fin thrust his hips at a frightening speed and came deep in Mick's ass. He collapsed between Mick's widely spread thighs, moved down his body, and swallowed his cock. He didn't even get a chance to do anything besides swallow it before Mick started shooting down his throat.

They were both almost asleep when Mick finally rolled out from under Fin and disappeared into the bathroom. Fin could hear the water in the sink running and then Mick came back to bed with a warm washcloth in his hand. He lovingly cleaned Fin's cock and threw the cloth onto the floor. They snuggled up together and drifted off to sleep.

Chapter Three

80

Mick's alarm went off four hours later. Mick swung his arm toward the clock and hit it until the buzzer stopped. He snuggled back up to the big muscular man beside him, burying his head in Fin's neck and nibbling softly. After each nibble Fin would get a soothing swipe of his tongue. Mick would be perfectly content to stay here all day, but he had to be downstairs in less than an hour to get the pub ready for business. He nipped Fin a little harder and reached for Fin's morning erection. "Mmm...you feel so nice and warm."

Fin cracked his eyes open and smiled at Mick. "What time is it?" He lazily thrust up into Mick's fist.

"Quarter after nine. Unfortunately it's time to get up. Although we might have time for a quick rub." He flashed his beautiful dimples at Fin.

Fin pulled him closer so they were both on their sides facing each other. He removed Mick's hand from his cock so their cocks could rub against each other and started moving. Fin gripped Mick's ass and kissed him deeply despite morning breath.

Mick rubbed his cock hard against Fin's. "You feel so good. I don't know if I'll ever get enough of you." He reached between them and pinched Fin's tightened nipples. Fin came, shooting so hard Mick actually felt the stream of cum spill onto his stomach and chest. Mick followed almost immediately, further soaking both bodies.

They continued to kiss and explore until they regained their strength. Mick sat up and swung his legs over the side of the bed. "Why don't you get in the shower first and I'll start breakfast. If we shower together we'll never get to work. As it is I'm not sure I'll be able to walk today." He looked over his shoulder at Fin and smiled.

Fin smiled back. "I'll be done in a couple minutes. Do you have some sweats or something I can borrow? I'll have to go home to get some clothes but the thought of putting on the stinky French fry clothes make me sick."

Mick laughed. "Sure, I've got some sweats you can borrow. I can't wait to see them on you. The pajama bottoms you wore last night were a gift from…a friend. They were two sizes too big for me but I didn't have the heart to throw 'em out." Mick stood and went to his dresser. He came back with a pair of black sweats and a gray t-shirt. "Maybe you could bring your suitcase over here. I mean, if you want to?"

Fin had a funny look on his face then gave his head a little shake. "Yeah, I'd like that." He got up and headed for the shower.

Mick wasn't sure what he'd said to put that look on Fin's face, but he knew he didn't like it. He went in to start breakfast. He got bacon and eggs out of the fridge, still thinking about Fin.

The bacon was all done by the time Fin came into the kitchen, his long curly hair still dripping water on his shirt. Mick had to smile at the snug fit of the sweats. "Damn, baby. Maybe you should keep those sweats."

Fin looked down at himself and shrugged. "I can fry the eggs while you take your shower."

Mick just nodded and headed for the shower. Fin's mood still hadn't improved. As he got into the shower it dawned on him, "Christ…Fin's jealous." Why hadn't he thought he might take the pajama bottom comment the wrong way? Mick washed his hair and did some heavy thinking. By the time he was dressed again, Mick knew he was going to have to be honest with Fin and tell him what no one else in Boston knew except Sean.

Fin was sitting at the table drinking a cup of coffee when Mick entered the room. He got up and got another cup of coffee for Mick and pulled the plates with eggs and bacon out of the warming oven.

Mick knew he was going to have to do this quickly or risk losing everything. He cleared his throat until he got Fin's attention. "I can tell something's wrong and I think I figured out what it is." He sat down at the kitchen table. "Does your mood have anything to do with the comment I made about the pajama bottoms coming from a friend?"

Fin looked down at his plate and picked at his eggs. "I know I don't have any right to feel jealous of someone in your past. Hell, this is the first time in my life I've ever even felt jealous. I'll get over it."

Mick reached across the table and took Fin's hand. "There's absolutely nothing to be jealous about." He squeezed Fin's hand a little tighter. "What I'm about to tell you no one else in Boston knows except Sean but I'm gonna trust you'll keep my secret." At Fin's nod, Mick sighed heavily. "Have you ever heard of Ian Gallagher?"

Fin looked at him like he was crazy. "Of course. He was one of the best tenors in the world before he vanished."

Mick smiled. "He didn't vanish. He decided to quit the world of music, cut his hair and move to Boston to live over a pub and become a bartender."

Fin jumped up, knocking his chair over in the process. "What! Are you tellin' me that you're Ian Gallagher?"

Mick laughed and shook his head. "No. I'm telling you that Ian Gallagher was the stage name for the tenor I used to be before I became a bartender."

Fin still looked confused. "I'm sorry, but I still don't understand. Why would you quit the music world to live over a pub and become a bartender?"

Mick stood up and hugged Fin. "It's a long story. Basically I became so famous and wealthy that I lost sight of what was important in my life. I lost the real reason I sang in the first place." Mick took a moment to get his thoughts in order. "I was raised poor. I already told you my dad took off when I was four. Well, after he left it was just me and my mom. She worked three part-time jobs to support us. We always had a roof over our head but little else. When my mom was home we'd sit on the couch at night and sing to entertain ourselves. What I'm about to say sounds like it belongs in a movie script but I swear on my mom's grave that it's the God's honest truth.

"One day when I was around fourteen I was sitting out on the fire escape singing to my mom and a music agent's car broke down right outside our building. He must've heard me singing because the next thing I knew he climbed up the fire escape and asked me to sign a contract with him on the spot. I saw it as a way for my mom and me to get out of the government housing we were living in. So I ended up signing with the agent and he made me rich and famous. Just what I'd thought I wanted."

Mick took a breath, trying to sort through his memories. "My mom never had to work another day. After about twelve years in the business I'd become obsessed with being famous. I couldn't earn money fast enough. My mother would call to talk to me and I'd be too busy going to the next concert to talk to her. One day I got a call from her saying she wasn't feeling well. I..." Mick stopped talking and wiped the tears from his eyes. "I told her to go to the doctor, that she could afford it. I was too busy to be bothered. My mother died of a brain aneurism two days later."

Fin kissed his forehead. "Oh, sweetheart, I'm so sorry."

Mick closed his eyes and held Fin even tighter. "I got the call right after coming off stage one night. That was the last time I ever sang for money. I fired my agent and canceled the remaining concert dates I still had open and moved back to Boston. I wandered into the pub one day. It was completely empty except a wise old bartender named Sean.

"I sat and talked to him for hours. Then I came back the next day and talked some more. He made me see that I had enough money to last a lifetime...that life was meant for living, not just for making money." Mick looked deep into Fin's green eyes. "He told me that he'd made a lot of mistakes in his life by thinking that success would equal love. He knew that he'd learned his lesson too late, but that there was still time for me. Sean offered me a job. I had nothing else to do so I jumped at it. It was the best decision I've ever made. Now when I sing for the crowd in the pub it's because I love it, not because someone's paying me." He kissed Fin softly. "The pajama pants were given to me as a gift from my agent. Not an ex-lover."

Fin kissed Mick again and blushed. "I'm sorry. You must think I'm some psycho to get jealous after only one night together."

"No, I don't think you're psycho. I've had nothing but short-term affairs and one-night stands my entire life. I've never asked someone to stay with me, Fin. Even after only one night with you I can honestly say I've never felt more for any man than I feel for you. I don't know what it is exactly that I'm feeling but it's very much there."

"Good, because I feel the same way." Fin kissed him again and headed toward the stairs. "I'm gonna sneak out now before Sally shows up for work. Would you mind if I'm late coming back? I've got to run my ten miles today and do a rotation on the weight machines at the gym. If I don't do it this morning I'll have to do it this evening and I was kinda hoping I'd be spending a nice evening on the couch with you."

Mick looked at the tight-fitting sweats again. "That sounds fine. Do what you need to do so that we can cuddle all evening."

Fin nodded and headed down the stairs.

* * * * *

The pub was pretty slow for a Sunday. Mick went ahead and told Sally she could go home if she wanted to. Jeff made a big pot of stew and some cornbread and went home too. At six o'clock Mick and Fin decided to close down for the night. They'd only had about thirty people all day.

Fin looked over at Mick, who was cleaning up behind the bar. "Is it always this dead on Sunday?" Fin picked up the last of the dirty glasses and headed toward the bar.

"Sometimes it is." He looked at Fin and smiled. "Except during football season. Then this place is packed."

Fin's eyebrows drew together. "You mean Da brings a TV into the pub to watch football?"

Mick laughed and picked up the remote control. "Watch." He pushed a button on the remote and a huge white screen slid down from the ceiling. Mick pushed another button and a data projector came on, showing the image onto the big white screen. Fin looked up at the ceiling. He hadn't even noticed the projection unit hanging there.

"How long has that been there?" Fin moved behind the bar to stand behind Mick.

Mick shrugged. "I don't know. Since I've been here anyway. Usually during the off-season Sean shows tapes of your old games." Mick reached back and pulled Fin's hips toward him.

Fin wrapped his arms around Mick and started brushing his cock against Mick's ass. He shook his head and put his head on Mick's shoulder. "I'm sorry. I just don't understand what's going on. What past games does Da have a tape of?"

Mick turned around and pulled Fin by the hand toward the office. "Come with me. I need to show you something." They entered Sean's office and Mick went over to the huge storage closet and unlocked the door. He opened the closet and stood back.

Fin hesitantly stuck his head in the closet. It was full of videotapes, shelves and shelves of nothing but videotapes. Fin walked into the closet to get a closer look. They were all labeled in his da's perfect handwriting. It looked like he had a videotape of every game Fin had ever played starting with his freshman year of high school and ending with the final game of last season.

Fin slowly reached out to touch one of the tapes. He couldn't believe he was really seeing this. He pulled down the tape from homecoming of his senior year in high school. Fin ran for five touchdowns that game. He pulled the tape into his chest and sat on the floor of the closet. He couldn't move, couldn't breathe. He felt wetness on his cheeks and realized he was crying.

Mick came to sit by him. Fin was wrapped in warm, comforting arms. He turned toward Mick and laid his head on top of Mick's. "Why? Why would my da treat me like he didn't even know I was alive for thirty years and do this?" Fin motioned to all the tapes. "I didn't think he'd ever even seen me play."

Mick reached up to dry Fin's tears. "I don't know, baby. That's something you need to discuss with him. All I know is a day doesn't go by that he doesn't talk about you in one way or another." He held Fin's face and kissed his eyes. "To be honest with you…until I met you I thought you must be a pretty ungrateful son. Then when I saw your reaction to the pictures on the walls I knew there was more to the story than I'd been aware of. Fin, you really need to clear the air with Sean before it's too late." Mick stopped abruptly like he'd said too much.

Fin pulled back a little and looked at him. "What are you saying? Is there something you're not telling me?"

Tears pooled in Mick's eyes. "I'm saying you need to talk to your da. Take it from me. You never know when tomorrows will run out." Mick pulled Fin in for a kiss. He licked the tears from Fin's face and kissed him passionately.

Fin set the videotape down and pulled Mick to him with both hands, bringing him onto his lap. He ran his hands down Mick's back to land on his ass. He kissed his jaw and worked his way down Mick's throat. He pulled the t-shirt over Mick's head and began to suck and bite his nipples. Fin was like a man possessed. He couldn't get enough. He turned and pushed Mick down on the floor of the closet and went to work on Mick's jeans.

Mick seemed to understand what Fin needed. He helped him by removing Fin's shirt and pants.

Fin hovered over him, supported by his strong biceps and forearms. He leaned down and ran his tongue over Mick's lips. "I wanna make love you, Mick." Fin sat back a little and dug in his jeans pocket, producing a small tube of lube. He held it up like he'd just found the prize in a box of cereal. "I had a feeling we might need this sometime today."

Mick ran his hands down Fin's chest and abdomen. Mick reached Fin's cock and looked at him. "Squirt some lube in my hand so I can lube you up while you stretch me."

Fin squirted a good-sized drop onto Mick's hand and put some on his own fingers. He spread Mick's legs even more and quickly stretched and lubed his ass while Mick stroked his cock. "I can't wait any more, sweetheart." Fin felt the head of his cock slowly breach the stretched muscles of Mick's ass. He felt the warmth surround his cock as he pushed in. Mick began moaning and thrusting up toward Fin's cock. Fin wanted Mick to feel every inch of his desire.

Fin liked making love to Mick like this, face-to-face. He stopped mid-stroke, suddenly aware of where his thoughts were going. Making love? Fin shook off the thought and continued his journey into Mick's ass. He liked the way Mick tightened his muscles around his cock, like he hated it every time Fin pulled out. He leaned down to run his tongue around the rim of Mick's lips. Mick's tongue snaked out and licked his tongue. Fin invaded Mick's mouth like a conquering hero. He licked every bit of Mick's mouth. He thrust his hips firmly but slowly. Fin didn't want a fast and furious fuck this time. He wanted to remember this moment for the rest of his life. It was the moment he finally got it. He finally understood why people were willing to go against their families and employers for the love of a good man. Most people see life in black and white but Fin and Mick were gray. Fin laughed out loud at his own pun.

Mick drew back a little and raised his eyebrows. "What's so funny?"

Fin leaned down to give him a quick kiss. "I'm not laughing at you, sweetheart. I was just thinking we're not gay, we're gray." He could tell Mick still didn't get it. "In a black-and-white world the two of us are gray."

Mick smiled and thrust his hips toward Fin's cock. "I'll be the gray in your world any day." Mick reached down to his own cock and started stroking, stopping every third stroke to gather pre-cum from the head. He caught his hand after one such collection of pre-cum and brought it to Fin's mouth. He licked Mick's palm clean and bent down to invade his mouth once more, sharing Mick's own essence with him. He continued his rhythm, pounding harder and faster as Mick looked into his eyes. When he felt his balls start to draw up he kissed Mick with all the passion in him. "I'm gonna come. Are you ready?"

"Bring it on," Mick said with a grin.

Fin buried himself as deeply as possible and shattered. Mick followed Fin, shooting an impressive stream of cum between them. He collapsed and rolled slightly to the side of Mick. He looked at Mick for a long time, unable to think about anything but the fear that was suddenly consuming him. He told himself he absolutely couldn't do this. Fin would not allow real emotions to get in the way of this month-long affair.

He rolled over and sat up. "I think we should move this upstairs. My da would die if he knew what we were just doing in his tape closet." Fin felt Mick's body tense, but it was gone in seconds.

Mick stood and held a hand down to Fin. "Come on, let's get a big bowl of stew and some cornbread and go upstairs and watch a movie."

* * * * *

Later that evening, with *Die Hard* playing on the television, the phone rang, waking the slumbering couple entwined on the deep couch. Mick got up and stood groggily, looking for the phone. He found it under the coffee table where it'd been kicked earlier in a moment of passion. He picked up the phone. "H-Hello?"

"Hey, Mick, it's Sean. How's everything goin' at the pub?"

Mick cleared his sleep-filled voice and blinked his eyes a little wider. "Hi, Sean. The pub's been good. We closed an hour early tonight. There's just not enough business on Sundays lately." Mick looked at the clock. It was eight-thirty which meant it was well after midnight in Ireland.

"Yeah but it'll pick up in another couple of months when football season starts up again."

Mick swallowed and closed his eyes at the reminder that Fin would soon be leaving him. "Yeah, you're right. What do you think about closing the bar on Sundays until then? It just doesn't seem worth the money to keep it open right now."

Sean blew out a breath. "I'll give it some thought. Speaking of thought... Have you seen much of Calder? I've tried calling the house for the past week but the machine always picks up."

Mick looked over at Fin, trying to determine whether he wanted to talk to his da. Fin shook his head no. "He's been spending a lot of time training and I saw him at the pub today. Could be he went out after we got off." Mick wagged his eyebrows at Fin. Fin repaid him by throwing a pillow at him. "Why are you up so late? Are you feeling okay?" Mick wanted to ask about his health but didn't want to give anything away with Fin in the room.

"Well, that's one of the reasons I called. I've been experiencing a bit of pain. I don't know if it's the cancer or all the walking I've been doing over here but I thought I'd see a doctor tomorrow just to be on the safe side. I wanted to know if you could go to the house and find my spare medical card and fax a copy to me. Mine has all but deteriorated in the wet weather over here. You might as well fax the medical file that I've been keeping. It's in the bottom drawer of my desk at home. It's not real technical but at least the doctor here will have an idea of what tests I've already had done and what medicines they've already tried."

Mick wondered how he was going to get away from Fin long enough to find and fax all the information Sean was asking for. "I'll see what I can do." Mick turned away from Fin and walked across the room. In an almost whispered voice Mick asked Sean a couple more questions. "Don't you think it would be better if you came on home? And what do I tell Fin if he wants to know why I've been in your house?"

Sean blew out a frustrated-sounding breath. "I've not finished yet what I set out to accomplish with this trip. I'll not be home until I think the task is complete. You can tell Fin I tripped and sprained my ankle and need my medical card faxed. That's what I was going to tell him. Of course if he were faxing the card I wouldn't have him send the medical file. I don't know, Mick…surely you can figure it out. Just don't tell him about the cancer yet."

Mick ran a hand through his hair in frustration at the stubborn man. "Okay, Sean. Do you want me to tell Fin anything if I see him?" Fin took the question as an invitation and lowered his sweats so his cock sprang free. Mick smiled and licked his lips.

"Tell him…" Sean began coughing into the phone. The coughs became so bad Mick was afraid they wouldn't stop. He gripped the phone tighter and willed his friend to stop.

"Tell him I love him and that I'm glad he's home where he belongs." Sean coughed a few more times. "I'll let you get back to whatever you were doing. Just fax the information as soon as you can to this number..." Sean read off his cousin's fax number and hung up, still coughing.

Mick turned to look at Fin again. God, how did he get in the middle of this? He was quickly distracted by the sight of Fin slowly stroking his erection. He looked like some kind of sultan lounging on the couch with fire in his eyes and his cock in his hand. Mick dropped the phone on the table and knelt beside the couch. He looked into Fin's eyes and then down at the throbbing cock in front of his face.

Fin ran his finger up the veins running along his cock and swiped a drop of moisture off the tip. He held his finger to Mick's lips, tempting him. Opening his mouth, Mick ran his tongue up the length of Fin's long tapered finger. Mick closed his mouth over the top, swallowing it down to the knuckle. He moaned at the taste exploding on his tongue. Mick pulled off the finger and looked into Fin's eyes.

"More. I want more of you. I'm going to suck your cock until you explode in my mouth and then I'm going to fuck your ass. I'm going to get so deep inside you you'll taste my cum in your mouth."

Fin leaned back on the sofa and parted his thighs. "I'm all yours, Mick. I have been since the first time I laid eyes on you. The thought of your mouth on my cock leaves me wanting more of you. My ass is twitching at the thought of your rigid cock in it. So come on, do your best."

Mick accomplished what he set out to do. He had Fin screaming so loudly by the time the ass fucking was over he thought Fin would be hoarse in the morning. Later, after their round of couch wrestling Mick led Fin into the bedroom and tucked him in.

41

He kissed Fin tenderly and looked into his dark green eyes. "I've got to go over to Sean's house and fax him a copy of his medical card. He's having a bit of chest pain, but he thinks it might be from all the walking he's done." He leaned down and kissed Fin again. "I won't be long. I'll wake you when I get home. We don't have to work tomorrow so we have all night to play."

Fin looked at Mick through narrowed eyes. "Why did Da ask you to fax the card?"

Mick ran his hands through Fin's dark curls. "He tried to call the house but for some reason the machine picked up. Could you think of any reason you wouldn't be at home?" He smiled. "Anyway he needs it faxed overnight. With the time difference and all it'll just be easier for him if I go and do it now."

Fin shook his head. "No, I'll go. He's my da and I've got a key to the house."

Mick smiled and kissed him. "I told Sean I'd do it. Besides I have a key to Sean's house. He gave it to me several years ago. Just go to sleep, Fin, and get your rest. The way my cock's already starting to notice you I think you'll need all the rest you can get."

* * * * *

Mick was back in bed within an hour. Fin was sleeping soundly so Mick decided to take the opportunity to just hold the man he was falling in love with. He didn't want to fall in love with him but it was quickly being taken out of his hands. Mick knew he couldn't lie to Fin about his da. That's why he told him that Sean was having chest pains. Not the complete truth but not a lie either.

With his arms wrapped around Fin he tried to decide the best course of action regarding Sean's well-kept secret. Fin had every right to know his da's time was short. What did Sean think he was saving Fin from? Was he afraid Fin would've tried to talk him out of his trip to Ireland? Everyone who was close to Sean knew he'd longed to go back to Ireland before he died.

Mick contemplated his choices. He could go against Sean's wishes and tell Fin or he could continue to keep the man he was falling in love with in the dark. As he turned over the choices in his head Mick slowly pulled back the sheet covering Fin's body. Fin was the embodiment of male perfection, a rugged warrior with a heart.

As the cool air hit his skin Fin shifted his position, searching for warmth. He found that warmth in Mick's body. Still asleep, Fin cuddled up to Mick's body and placed his hand on Mick's cock which went rigid in a heartbeat. He continued to study Fin's body. With just a sprinkling of black hair across his chest most of Fin's muscles were clearly defined. Mick knew how hard Fin worked to keep his body in this kind of condition. He suddenly felt guilty, wishing Fin would give up the life he worked so hard for and stay in Boston with him.

Mick circled Fin's nipples and watched the tiny nubs protrude like they were searching for his kiss. He decided to obey the unspoken invitation and bent his head and took the nub into his mouth. He licked and flicked his tongue over the growing protrusion and took it between his teeth, biting down gently. Fin groaned in his sleep and his hand started an unconscious rhythm of stroking Mick's cock. As Fin opened his eyes opened his eyes Mick looked at the sleepy face and couldn't resist placing a soft kiss on Fin's sleep-swollen lips.

Mick's eyes rolled into the back of his head and he gently thrust upward. He reached his own hand down to the base of Fin's rising cock. He stroked Fin's perfect cock like it was the softest kitten fur. Mick reached farther down and ran his hands over Fin's heavy scrotum, rolling the balls in his hand.

Fin thrust toward him and slowly opened his eyes. "Mmmm…more." Fin began a more thorough investigation of

Mick's cock as he continued to thrust his own toward Mick's hand. "So hot, sweetheart."

Mick climbed on top of Fin and rubbed his now-dripping cock along his abdomen, leaving pearly white tracks in his wake. "I wanna ride you, Fin."

"Mmmm…" Fin groaned and positioned Mick over his cock. He reached toward the bedside table and got out the bottle of lube. "Gotta slick you up first." Fin dribbled the lube over his own erection and began sliding Mick back and forth over his cock. The feel of Mick's ass cheeks enveloping his cock was heaven. "Gonna come if you don't climb on."

Mick rose slightly off Fin. His ass thoroughly lubed, he positioned the soft pucker of his ass above Fin's cock and as he held the cock in position, he lowered himself. The minute Fin's cock breached his entrance he was lost in an orgasmic high. He came in a spurt onto Fin's chest before he was fully seated on the huge cock. "Sorry, baby. You feel so good…oh God…yes!"

Fin smiled and took over. Thrusting his cock up into Mick's ass, he finally flipped them over so he could get on top. Fin needed to fuck Mick hard. He repositioned Mick's thighs and put them over his shoulders. Lining up his cock again, he pushed home—and that's exactly what Mick's ass felt like to him, home. He drove past the ring of muscles and all the way to the root in one thrust.

Mick was coming out of his pleasure haze and reached up to hold the headboard. "Harder. Fuck me harder." He pulled his legs off Fin's shoulders and brought them over his own head to touch the headboard with his feet. This gave Fin what he needed to go deeper into his ass. Fin fucked Mick harder and faster than he'd ever been fucked in his life. "Too much…oh Fin, gonna come again."

With the position he was currently in, his cock stabbed into his chest with every thrust of Fin's hips. "Gonna shoot myself in the eye, Fin." Mick smiled when Fin looked down at him, shocked. He saw that indeed Mick's cock was lined up with his face and laughed.

"Damn, that's sexy. Shoot in your own mouth, Mick. I wanna see it." Fin's words seemed to spur his own orgasm because after a couple more deep, hard thrusts he was howling his release.

Mick grabbed his own cock and exploded toward his face, catching most of his seed on his cheek but getting a few strands to land in his own mouth. "Mmm...I taste good," Mick said with a chuckle and a wink.

Fin let go of Mick's legs and rolled to the side, keeping his chest over Mick's. He leaned down and licked Mick's face clean and then delved into his mouth for a scorching kiss. He broke the kiss and laid a hand on the side of Mick's face. "You've always tasted good to me."

"Must be all the fruit juice I drink. No wonder you enjoy sucking my cock so much." He ran his hands down the side of Fin's torso to the globe of one cheek and squeezed. He looked into Fin's face and couldn't stop his next words. "I'm falling in love with you and I'm afraid."

Fin lowered his head and rested it in Mick's neck. "I know, me too. I have to leave in another three weeks for preseason training. I've never tried a long-distance relationship. Hell, I've never tried a relationship. Maybe I could try getting traded to the Patriots?"

Mick shook his head slowly from side to side. "You could never play for the Patriots and still have a relationship with me. I won't be hidden away like a dirty little secret for the next few years. I understand the importance of it as far as your career but I can't live that way. Nor could I relocate to New York to be with you. As long as you play football you just aren't free to be with me."

Fin kissed him enjoying the lingering taste of Mick's seed. "Football is my life. It's the only thing I've ever been good at. Who am I without it?"

Mick pulled Fin closer, wrapping his leg around Fin's thigh. "You're the man I love. I don't love you because you can play football. I love you because you make me laugh. You're big and strong, but you have this inner core about you that is soft and tender. You're a wonderful man. Why would you sell yourself short?"

Fin shrugged his shoulders and traced Mick's leanly muscled chest with his fingers. "Since the seventh grade football's the only thing people want to talk to me about. It's become almost my entire identity."

Mick kissed the top of Fin's head. "You're wrong. Football doesn't define who you are. Your generous heart does that. Did you ever think that maybe people have always just been drawn to you? That maybe football was the only thing they could talk to you about because they knew it was a subject that you enjoyed? Could it possibly be that the people around you feel inferior not superior to you and talking to you about football makes them feel closer to you?"

Fin's hand stopped its movement on Mick's chest. "No...I never considered any of those things. Why would anyone in the world feel inferior to me?"

Mick sighed. "Maybe because you're a warm, caring, incredibly hot stud who also happens to play professional football for New York. I'd never ask you to give up your career if it's something you love doing, but I'm beginning to question why you even play. Do you love the game or do you love the admiration? Whether you play or not you're still admirable...because you're Calder Finnegan."

He watched as Fin's eyes filled with tears before quickly being blinked away.

"I need some time. Will you love me anyway?"

Mick laughed and rolled over on top of Fin. "I've no choice in the matter. If I did I might never have fallen in love with you in the first place. Nothing about this is going to be easy but nothing good ever is. I'll stand by you and accept whatever decisions you make."

"Thank you."

Chapter Four

ള

Monday morning Mick opened his eyes and stretched his overworked muscles. One thing he could say for sure was that he'd sure gotten his share of exercise the last two days. He looked at the clock. It was only ten after eight. Wow, Mick thought to himself, he couldn't remember the last time he'd gotten up this early. He looked over at Fin and smiled. Spread-eagled on the bed, Fin looked like a beautiful sacrifice.

He scratched at his five o'clock shadow and thought about what he'd like to do on his only day off. Mick decided to take a leap of faith and share something special with Fin. He leaned over and softly kissed Fin's lips before moving on to his neck and then up to his ear. He slowly sucked the lobe into his mouth as Fin groaned.

"Mmm...I'll give you an hour to stop that." Fin cracked an eye and smiled at Mick.

"As much as the thought appeals to me I've decided we need to take a trip up the coast for the day. So get up and get dressed." Mick smacked Fin on the ass. "The day's a-wastin'." Mick jumped out of bed and headed for the shower. He knew Fin would soon follow and they'd never get out of the shower let alone the house. Mick quickly washed his hair and soaped himself down and stepped out of the shower. He decided to give his skin a break and go with the scruffy look and not shave. He quickly brushed his teeth and was just coming out of the bathroom as Fin was coming in.

Fin stopped and looked at him in confusion. "Hey, what's goin' on? I was just gonna join you."

Mick wrapped his arms around Fin's neck and kissed him. "I know, that's why I hurried. I want to share something

47

with you and we've got to get going." He gestured to the shower. "So hop in and hop out. I'll go find something quick for breakfast." He kissed Fin one more time and slapped him on the ass. "Get a move on, baby."

* * * * *

It was a beautiful May day and Fin was enjoying the drive up the coast. The air smelled so much better here than in Manhattan. That's one of the things he hated most about the city. You could never just wake up and go outside and take a deep breath of clean morning air.

He still lived in the small one-bedroom condo he'd bought when he'd signed his first contract. He had enough money to buy a mansion like a lot of players in the NFL but it just didn't make sense to him. He didn't have any friends who came over and Lord knows he didn't date, so it was just him. Why spend the money when he didn't care and no one else did either?

Fin turned his head slightly against the headrest and looked at Mick. God, he was magnificent. His profile was absolutely perfect like it'd been carved from marble. He reached out a hand and brought it down on Mick's thigh. Mick squeezed his thighs together, essentially squeezing him back.

Fin smiled and Mick turned his sultry blue eyes his way. "Not much farther. Only about another twenty minutes."

"Why don't you at least tell me where we're going?"

Mick smiled and turned the radio down. "Then it wouldn't be a surprise. I'm about to share something that no one else knows about. Not even Sean. Which is really saying a lot because I think Sean knows most of my secrets. This one I've held to myself for nine years."

Fin ran his hand over Mick's jeans-covered cock. "Are you sure there isn't a way I can convince you to tell me your secret now?"

Mick put his hand on top of Fin's and thrust his cock upward. "Nice try, but this secret you have to see in person."

Twenty minutes later Mick pulled up to an iron gate and keyed in a number on the touch pad. The gate opened slowly to reveal a long driveway. Mick steered his SUV down the winding drive and pulled up in front of a faded gray-shingled three-story house that sat on a bluff overlooking the Atlantic Ocean.

The house took Fin's breath away. It was absolutely picturesque. A wide porch wrapped around the entire house. Flower boxes filled with red geraniums sat underneath each window and in large pots beside the porch steps. It was a beautiful house on the most perfect bluff he'd ever seen. "I'm in awe of this place." He turned to look at a smiling Mick. "Is it yours?"

Mick got out of the car and went around opening Fin's door. "Yes, this house is mine. It's the only thing I kept after I quit the music business. It's where I lived when I met Sean."

Fin looked at him like he was crazy. "You left this wonderful house to live above an Irish pub? If this were my house I'd never leave." Fin gave a quick bark of laughter. "I'd even have my groceries delivered."

Mick wrapped his arm around Fin and looked out over the ocean. "It's got everything a man could want—except companionship. After I quit the business I moved here and didn't leave for almost six months. Yeah, I even had my groceries delivered. I needed to figure out who I was and what I wanted from the rest of my life. I finally figured it out. I wanted the same as any man. A job I could be proud of, a home that felt warm and safe, good friends and someone to love. Although I never even hoped that I could feel the kind of love I feel for you."

Mick looked at Fin and ran his palm down the side of Fin's face. "You complete my life. You're the missing piece of the puzzle." He smiled and started dragging Fin toward the front door. "Come on, I'll show you around."

They went up the steep front porch steps and Mick unlocked the door. "I have a woman who comes twice a week to water the flowers and do light housekeeping so it shouldn't be too bad in here."

Fin walked into the beautifully decorated house. "Why do you need a cleaning woman twice a week if you never come up here to get it dirty?"

Mick shrugged. "I like the flowers out front. When I do come up the flowers make me smile. Watering the flowers didn't require enough hours to get someone to come over twice a week so I found Hildy and asked if she would keep the dust down inside as well."

Fin opened a set of French doors that led out to the side of the house with the ocean view. He walked to the rail and took a deep breath. He could smell fresh cut grass and ocean. Fin closed his eyes. "Does Hildy know who you were?"

Mick came to stand behind him. He wrapped his arms around Fin's waist and leaned his head on Fin's back. "No. She knows Dominic Sullivan owns this house. She doesn't know I'm Ian Gallagher." He kissed Fin's neck. "Before a couple of days ago, only Sean and my agent knew that Dominic Sullivan and Ian Gallagher were the same man. My agent died a year ago, which just left Sean, until you."

Fin turned around and put his arms around Mick. "Thank you again for trusting me with your secret."

Mick kissed him. "Enough serious stuff. I brought you here to have fun. Let me show you my pride and joy." Mick led Fin toward the back of the house. He stopped outside a locked door. "This room will probably be very dusty. I keep it locked so Hildy doesn't figure out my secret." Mick unlocked the door and stepped inside.

Fin walked in behind Mick. "A recording studio? Man, that's so cool. Do you still record songs?" Fin walked over to the wall littered with gold and platinum records.

Mick dusted off a stack of CDs and looked at Fin. "Yeah, I still record. But I record only Irish ballads now. The difference is now I do it for myself and the enjoyment I get out of it. Not for the money or the fame."

Fin shuffled his feet and bit his cheek. "Um…would it be too much to ask for a copy of one of your CDs? I'd like to take it back to New York with me. I won't let anyone else hear it but I…well…I can play it when I'm missing the sound of your voice."

Mick took the pile of CDs off the shelf and began looking through them. He selected one and handed it to Fin. "This is nothing but Irish love songs, slow and sweet. If I'm going to be talking to you through my music I'd like it to be through these songs." Mick put his head down and left the room.

Fin looked around one more time and fingered the CD case in his hand. He knew how Mick felt. Hell, he was feeling the same way but what choice did he have? His football career was his whole life, wasn't it? Fin shook off the thought and went to find Mick.

Mick was in the kitchen putting something in the oven. Fin walked in and put his hand on Mick's back. "Hey. Are we all right?"

Mick turned and wrapped his arms around him. "Please just tell me to stop borrowing trouble. I know you're going to leave but I can't stop getting angry about it. I just found you. I've searched my entire life for you and it hurts to know I have to let you go in another three weeks."

Brushing his hands over Mick's back, Fin kissed his forehead. "I know, sweetheart. I'm just sick about the whole situation. I can only promise that I'll be here for you if you ever need me. Just because I have to go back to New York doesn't mean I'll stop loving you. I'll gladly continue a long-distance relationship if that's what you want, but for another few years my career is in New York."

Carol Lynne

Mick pulled away and went back to the stove. "I'm heating up a casserole that Hildy left in the freezer." He checked the casserole and shut the oven door. Turning back to Fin, he just stared at him for a few seconds. "I'll need time to think about the whole staying in the closet thing. Right now I'm tempted to bounce up and down and say yes, but I'm not sure what that would do to our relationship in the long run. I want to make the best decision for both of us...okay?"

Fin walked toward Mick and pulled him back into his arms. "That's all I can ask of you. Just know that I'll be thinking too." He bent his head and kissed Mick passionately, eating his mouth from the inside. The kiss ignited Fin's cock and he moved closer to Mick, slowly rubbing his cock against the hard bulge in Mick's soft faded jeans. When Mick grabbed his ass he knew they were on the same page.

Mick started pulling off Fin's faded gray t-shirt and pants. "No more talk...just love me." Mick ran his tongue down over Fin's jaw to his neck. He traced the bulging tendon and continued to his shoulders, where he touched with his fingers and tongue. Mick inched downward, mapping Fin's body with his hands and mouth, as though he was trying like hell to imprint every freckle, every hair and every bulging muscle.

Mick nipped the sharp defined ridges of Fin's abdomen and swirled his tongue inside his belly button. Fin seemed to understand Mick's needs and just let him explore. Mick moved his hands to Fin's hard muscled butt and took a pale globe in each hand. He nipped at Fin's hipbones and finally moved in, burying his face in Fin's black nest of curls. He inhaled deeply and sighed. He moved his lips lower and kissed the head of Fin's throbbing cock. Snaking his tongue out, Mick dipped into the slit in the top. He closed his eyes, savoring Fin's taste on his tongue. He knew no matter what, he would never forget this day, this moment.

Fin began to thrust his cock down Mick's throat until he put his hands on Mick's head to hold him and felt the tears. He stopped and immediately pulled out of Mick's throat and fell

52

to his knees to hold him. Mick couldn't get control of his emotions and began to shake in Fin's arms.

Fin held Mick's face and tilted it upward so he could see his eyes. He kissed away a few trickling tears from beneath Mick's long black eyelashes. "Sweetheart? Did I hurt you?"

Mick just stared at him for a few seconds, then shook his head and buried his face in Fin's chest once again. "This... This feeling. It's what life's all about. Just hold me. That's all I need right now is for you to hold me." Mick hung on to Fin's neck like he was drowning.

Fin lifted Mick and carried him out to the porch. He found an Adirondack chair and sat down, settling Mick on his lap. Mick put his head down on Fin's shoulder and continued to hold on. Fin looked out over the porch railing to the Atlantic Ocean beyond. He ran his palm up and down Mick's back. "It's okay, I'm here. I've got your back."

They sat like that for a long time, eventually then eventually Mick settled down and kissed Fin's neck. "I'm sorry that happened. I can't even tell you why because I'm not sure I completely understand it. I was trying my best to imprint you into my mind and heart and the emotions were so true, so...beautiful...that I felt overwhelmed with love for you." Mick shook his head. "Can we just stay like this for a while longer?"

Fin kissed the top of his head. "I'd say yes but the timer for the casserole went off about fifteen minutes ago and I'm starting to smell smoke. Let me go in and take it out of the oven. I'll find something in the fridge that I can feed you. How does that sound?"

"Good, but it would be even better if you brought a blanket back out with you. The ocean breeze is about to freeze my bits and pieces off." He winked at Fin.

Chapter Five

🔊

They spent the remainder of the day outside. First on the porch where Fin fed both of them lunch and then later in the evening they took the blanket out to the bluff overlooking the ocean. They spooned their bodies together and just talked about nothing and everything.

Mick turned around to face Fin. He reached out and gently tucked an errant curl behind his ear. "Thank you for today. Honestly…it's been one of the best days of my life."

"You're welcome. The only thing that could make this day any better would be a beautiful Irish love ballad sung by a gorgeous Irish tenor to the equally gorgeous Irish man he loves." Fin smiled and kissed him.

Mick looked at Fin and narrowed his eyes. "You actually want me to perform for you?"

Fin shook his head. "No. I want you to make love to me with your voice. I'm just sorry you don't play the fiddle. There's nothing better than a love song with a slow fiddle in the background."

Mick winked and sighed. "I'll sing to you all day, but I'll never play the fiddle again."

Fin held him a little tighter. "Would you tell me why?"

Mick put his head on Fin's chest and sighed. "My mom taught me how to play when I was just a boy. Every evening we'd practice the fiddle and sing. When I signed with my agent he told me not to play the fiddle with my music. He thought it would bring a lower-class perception to my image."

Mick shrugged his shoulders. "I was young and didn't care what I had to give up to become rich and famous.

54

Throughout my entire career, I wasn't allowed to play the fiddle in public. When my mom died and I came home to Boston for her funeral and I knew I was finished with the music business. So the evening after the funeral I went back to the cemetery and played the fiddle for my mom. I vowed to her that all the love she'd put into my magic fiddle I would give back to her in song. I played for hours that night and I filled my fiddle with all the grief I had in me. I haven't played the fiddle since. It holds nothing but grief and sadness for me now."

Fin pulled him closer and wiped a tear from his eye. "Thank you for telling me. I understand why you don't play it now. I only wish I'd known you then. I wish I could've met your mom…she sounds like a beautiful lady."

Mick kissed Fin's chest. "She was the most beautiful person in the world…inside and out." Mick was silent for a long time and then, softly at first, he began to sing.

* * * * *

They drove back to Boston the following morning in companionable silence. Mick held his hand the entire ride. Fin was glad Mick loved him enough to show him his house and to share another memory of his mother, even though it was painful. Fin looked out the window and yawned.

Mick looked over toward him and smiled. "Keep you up too late, did I?" He squeezed Fin's hand a little tighter.

Fin smiled back at him. "It was worth losing sleep over, believe me. I was just thinking about the long day ahead. I don't know how Da did it all these years. I'm tired after only a couple of weeks."

Mick brought Fin's hand to his mouth and kissed his knuckles. "I think in the beginning he didn't have a choice. From what I hear the pub didn't really start making much of a profit until recently. Sean couldn't afford to hire the people he really needed and still make a profit. So he did most of the work himself."

Mick looked over at Fin. "You need to talk to him. He knows he screwed up at being a dad but he needed the bar to support his family. As you grew up he realized that making enough money for the nice house and private school wasn't worth losing his family over but it was too late. You'd already grown apart to the point that he felt you resented him so he just kept staying away. I think staying away was easier for him than to come to you and admit he'd made a lot of mistakes. That's another thing I've learned about Sean…too much damned pride."

Fin noticed how Mick spat out the last few words but he figured maybe Mick had gone a few rounds with Sean over something that wasn't his business. "I know I should talk to him. Before I came back here I was just too bitter to hold much of a conversation with him but now that I've seen the office and storeroom…" Fin was silent for a few seconds. "I'm still not sure I understand what that stuff is all about."

Mick looked in his rearview mirror and pulled the car over to the side of the road. He turned his body in the seat to face Fin. He took Fin's chin in his hand and pulled it to face him. "Don't you get it yet? Sean didn't miss a single one of your games. He may not have been able to be there physically, but he made damned sure he was able to see them anyway. He's killed himself at that bar for over thirty years and in his mind he did it because he loved you and your mother. He was wrong to do it the way he did and he knows that now. Give the man a second chance to be the kind of father you always wanted." Mick knew he'd said too much but damn it, Fin needed to make peace with Sean before it was too late. If he had to explain the things Sean should have explained years ago then so be it.

Mick leaned over and kissed Fin. "I don't mean to get in the middle of you and Sean but I love you and I love your da. I can't stand the two of you being at odds anymore."

Fin kissed him back and nodded. "I'll think about what you said. That's all I can promise right now in regards to my da."

* * * * *

The bar was busy for a Wednesday evening. Of course it was summer so the college kids partied like every night was a Friday night. It had been just as bad last night. Fin was helping Mick at the bar when a guy of about twenty-three came up to order a drink. Fin looked up and saw that Mick was building a Guinness. "What can I get for you tonight?"

The guy looked up and his jaw dropped down. "Oh…oh my God…you're Calder Finnegan. I've watched you play for years. You're like my favorite player. What are you doing tending bar?"

Fin knew it would eventually happen. He'd been damn lucky so far that most people if they did know who he was just didn't give a shit. Fin decided to smile and be polite. "My da owns this pub. I'm helping out while he's in Ireland."

"Damn. If more people knew you were in Boston this place would be packed every night. Why don't you advertise it or something?"

Fin shrugged his shoulders. "It's the off-season and I'm just helping out my da. I'm not trying to get publicity. What can I get you to drink?"

Fin caught Mick watching him from the other end of the bar. He knew the drink orders were starting to back up but he couldn't seem to get rid of this guy.

"Tell me…how did it feel to score four times in one game?"

"It was a good feeling. Now, I'm getting behind in the drink orders, is there anything I can get you?"

"Why? Do you think you're too good to talk to a fan?" The guy started to get loud and Fin could see Mick heading his way down the bar.

"I'm just trying to tend bar here, guy. Please give me your drink order or step away from the bar."

The guy became enraged at Fin's request and blindsided Fin with a punch to the side of the head. Unfortunately the guy had a big gold class ring on that split the skin on Fin's cheekbone. Fin's head was thrown back at the punch and when he righted himself he saw Mick leap across the bar.

Mick grabbed the guy by the hair and started pulling him out of the bar. Fin had to give it to Mick, he may be lean, but, damn, he was strong. The guy ended up tripping over a chair but that didn't stop Mick from dragging him by the hair out of the pub. Mick closed the front door and talked to a couple of the regulars up front and pointed to the door.

Mick practically ran back up to and over the bar. He grabbed a clean bar rag and wet it down, bringing it over to Fin. Fin tried to take the rag but Mick ignored him.

He cleaned the cut and then held the rag in place. By this time Fin was the focus of every eye in the bar. Mick leaned toward him to talk into his ear. "You need a couple of stitches in this, baby. I'll have Joe drive you over to the hospital."

Mick started to walk off but Fin stopped him. "I'm not going to the hospital. Just send Joe to find a pharmacy and get a package of butterfly bandages. I'm a football player, for God's sake. I get cut up all the time. Believe me, all I need is a butterfly bandage on it and it'll heal even better than stitches. I promise."

Mick removed the rag again and looked at the cut. "Okay, fine, but I'm sending you upstairs and I'm closing up early. I don't like the tension in here right now anyway." Mick walked off and went to speak with Joe, one of the regulars. Joe nodded and finished his beer and left.

Mick came back to the bar and stood on top of it. "May I have your attention please? I'm sorry, ladies and gentlemen, but the pub will be closing early tonight. You have thirty minutes to finish your drinks. I'm sorry for any inconvenience and I hope you'll all come back to Finnegan's."

Mick jumped off the bar to nods and a few grumbles. He walked back over to Fin. "I thought you were going upstairs?"

Fin shook his head. "I'm fine, Mick. I'll stay and help you get these people out. After all, it's my fault all these people have to leave early. The least I can do is stay and thank them for coming in. Besides, I don't trust that asshole to stay away. I'm not leaving you to close up by yourself and that's final."

Fin didn't want Mick to know it, but he was feeling a little lightheaded so he went and sat down in the kitchen. Joe came back with the bandages and Mick brought them back to him.

He stood over Fin and opened the package, taking two bandages out. Mick went to the first-aid cabinet and got an alcohol swab to clean the cut. He positioned himself so that he could easily work on the cut. Unfortunately that position was too much temptation for Fin.

Mick was basically straddling Fin's thigh even though he was still standing. Mick opened the alcohol swab. "I'm sorry, but this is gonna sting." He cleaned the cut with gentle touches and then blew on it just like Fin's mom used to do.

Fin began to get distracted by the sight of Mick's half hard cock. He raised his knee just enough to brush against the crotch of Mick's jeans. Mick jumped and looked into his eyes. "Be careful what you're doin', Fin. I'm getting ready to put this bandage on and if I don't get it right you could end up with a nasty little scar." His words were serious but then he ruined it by winking and rubbing his now-hard cock against Fin's knee.

Mick put the first bandage on then opened the second. While he was pulling off the tabs, Fin was busy caressing his cock. Mick breathed deeply and managed to concentrate enough to get the second bandage on before he let out a moan. "Give me ten more minutes to clear the bar and then I'll be back to ride your little pony."

Fin laughed. "Little pony, my ass. You'll be riding a Clydesdale." Mick walked off laughing.

Ten minutes later Mick was back. He stopped in the doorway. Fin smiled to himself. No longer was he merely sitting on the stool but now he was completely naked. He grinned at Mick. Mick rubbed the hard ridge behind his fly. "Fuck, you're sexy."

Fin crooked his finger at him. "C'mere, Dr. Sullivan, I'm in need of some more medical attention."

Mick rolled his eyes and started taking off his clothes. "Is that right and just what is the nature of your condition, sir?" Mick sauntered up to Fin's side.

Fin took Mick's hand and lowered it to his erection. "I've got swelling and I need you to help alleviate it. Can you do something, Doc?"

Mick grabbed a bottle of vegetable oil and sat on Fin's lap. "Oh, I might know of a thing or two but it might take a more thorough examination. I may even have to do a complete workup on you."

Fin took the bottle from Mick and poured some oil onto his fingers. He stretched his own legs wider, which in turn, spread Mick's out wider. He reached behind Mick and started spreading the oil around Mick's hole. Mick leaned forward, burying his face in Fin's black curls.

Leaning back into Fin's touch, Mick moaned. "Enough. Want you in me."

Withdrawing his fingers, Fin positioned his cock and Mick impaled himself. "Oh God. Yes." Fin lifted Mick just enough that he could thrust in and out at lightning speed. The burn of his muscles added to the overall atmosphere of rough and raw fucking. He withdrew his cock and lifted Mick to his feet. Fin stood and bent Mick over the chair and slammed into him again and again.

The heat of Mick's hole had Fin soon breaking out into a sweat. "Damn, hot…tight and hot." He ground his staff as far as it would go in Mick's tight heat and shot his seed deep inside his love. Wrapping his hand around Mick's cock, Fin stroked him to completion. The splash of heat on his hand felt like fire.

They collapsed back into the chair, Mick cuddled up to him, life was good today. He looked into Mick's baby blue eyes and kissed him. "Love you."

"Mmm…" Mick snuggled closer, rubbing his cheek against Fin's chest. They were getting ready to clean up when the phone rang. Mick slipped his jeans on and went behind the bar to the phone.

"Finnegan's." Mick watched while Fin cleaned his cock with a rag and pulled his jeans on.

"Mick?"

"Hey, Sean. How'd it go yesterday?"

"Mick…I have to come home. The cancer's spread and they think if I don't leave the country now I won't be healthy enough to make it home at all."

"Damn."

"Yeah. Look, I need you to pick me up at the airport Friday night at eight-thirty. Have you seen Fin?"

Mick swallowed around the lump in his throat. Oh God, he so could not cry in front of Fin. "Yeah, he's here with me at the pub."

"Have you two gotten close enough that you could tell him why I'm coming home? I've tried to…I just can't do it. I was hoping you two had gotten on well enough that you could ease him into it before I got there."

Mick closed his eyes. How could he tell the man he loved that his da was coming home to die? "Fuck, Sean. I don't think you know what you're asking of me."

"Yeah. I think I do. I'll...uh...see you Friday night. Tell Fin...tell Fin I love him, would you?"

Mick shook his head, suddenly angry with his old friend. "No, I won't tell him. That's a job you should have taken care of yourself a long time ago. I won't get you out of that one. So swallow your pride and tell the man how you feel." He looked up as Fin started to walk toward him. "Before it's too late."

"I'll see you Friday night. Bye. And...thanks."

Sean hung up and Mick stood frozen with the phone still clenched in his hand. He put his head down so Fin couldn't see the tears swimming in his eyes. He was so lost in his own anger and hurt he didn't even hear Fin walking up to him. He let Fin take the phone out of his hand and hang it up. Mick still couldn't look up.

Fin wrapped his arms around Mick and kissed the top of his head. "What is it, sweetheart? Who was on the phone that's got you so upset?" Fin ran his hands up and down Mick's back.

Looking up into Fin's beautiful green eyes, Mick kissed him. "Sean. It was Sean on the phone. He's...coming back to the States Friday night. He needs us to pick him up from the airport at eight-thirty."

Pulling back a little, Fin tilted his head sideways. "Why's Da coming back so early? Does this have something to do with his chest pain?"

Mick nodded. "Take me up to bed and I'll tell you all about it. I need to be home...not in the pub." Fin nodded and led Mick up the stairs to his loft. Fin got them both undressed and put Mick into bed.

Mick was grateful that Fin locked up and turned off the lights before sliding into bed next to him. Fin wrapped his arms around Mick and pulled him to his chest. "Talk to me, sweetheart."

Burying his face in Fin's neck, Mick felt like his lips were completely numb. Like all the tears and pain had moved to his lips making them too swollen to talk. "I…I don't know how to tell you this, so I'm just going to say it. Sean has lung cancer. He's getting worse and he's coming home to die." Tears escaped down Mick's cheeks.

"I'm sorry I didn't tell you but I promised Sean I'd let him do it when he got back. What you heard downstairs was me angry with him because he's a fucking coward. He asked me to tell you before he flew in. If I'd known I was going to be the one to do his dirty work I'd have done it sooner. I don't want you to think I was keeping a secret from you. It just wasn't my secret to tell…until that phone call downstairs just now."

Fin said nothing. He felt like someone had knocked the wind out of his sails. Mick continued to kiss his neck and stroke his chest but he felt…nothing. He slowly got out of bed and put his jeans on. He started walking toward the door despite Mick's pleas to stay. He walked out of the loft and down the stairs to his da's office and locked the door. Fin opened the door to the storage room and went in, shutting the door behind him, sliding to the floor in a heap.

Fin didn't know how long he'd sat there with his arms wrapped around his legs but he vaguely remembered Mick pounding on his da's office door, yelling for him to open it and let him in. Fin didn't know whether he wanted to let anyone in, ever.

He rocked back and forth, leaning his head on his knees. He needed to think. He needed to cry or smash something, but all he could do was rock. He'd had such hopes after seeing this room. Maybe his da really was proud of him. Maybe they could start over and share things the way most fathers and sons did.

How long had his da known about the cancer? Was he such a bad son that his da didn't think it was important to tell him? Didn't he want to spend what time he had left with Fin? The more he sat there the more questions he had. Fin knew most of the answers would have to come from his da but he could get a few answers now from Mick.

Maybe he could fly his da to another doctor. Hell, it wasn't like he didn't have the money. There had to be something they could do to fix him. What was the point of having money if you couldn't do something good with it? His da's life was worth a hell of a lot more than some stupid mansion or sports car. That's what he'd have to do. He'd get his da the very best doctors in the country even if he spent every penny he had doing it. With his new resolve, Fin decided it was time to talk to Mick.

Damn Mick for not telling him. But Mick would never betray Sean's trust. It was one of the things he loved about the man. Shit, he felt so alone and confused.

Fin got up off the floor and opened the storage room door. Looking back over his shoulder, he shook his head at all the tapes. All moments in time he wished he could have shared with his da. Fin turned out the light and walked away. He stood at the office door, trying to decide what he wanted next. The answer came to him with barely a thought—Mick, he needed Mick.

He opened the door to find Mick on the floor in front of the office, trembling. Fin walked over and picked him up, cradling him in his arms. He turned and walked up the stairs with Mick's body held tightly in his arms. He carried Mick to the bedroom and laid him down. Crawling in beside him, he didn't bother removing any clothes, he just needed to hold Mick.

Fin reached over to the bedside table and pulled off the box of tissues. He handed one to Mick and put the box up by the headboard. Mick blew his nose and motioned for another one. He blew his nose again then looked up at Fin.

"I failed you. Like I failed my mom. I'm so sorry I didn't tell you. God, I'm so sorry…"

Fin felt a tear slide down his own cheek. Not for his da or for him but for Mick. "I'm sorry I left. I...I just needed to take it all in. I don't blame you for this. I love you."

Mick reached for another tissue and blew his nose again. "Do you have any questions for me? I mean, I'd rather you asked your da but I understand the need to know some things now." He curled his body around Fin's.

"How long has Da known about this and has he tried any sort of treatment? Maybe the doctors could still help him. I've just been thinking about finding him a more qualified cancer specialist." Fin stroked Mick's head, trying his best to calm him down.

Mick shook his head and sighed. "He found out about eight months ago. He underwent chemotherapy and a round of radiation but nothing helped. I'm sorry but another doctor won't help him now. Medically, there's nothing they can do for him anymore. I tried to get him to call you but he said it was the middle of the football season and you had your own life to lead."

Mick kissed Fin's naked chest. "I didn't know you then and I felt Sean needed to make the decision when to inform you. I've been on his ass for months about telling you but he said he had a reason for everything. He thought he had another six months before he would start to get really sick but I think maybe that timeline is out the window now."

Fin shook his head. "How did he get lung cancer? Da's never smoked a day in his life."

"He's worked in a pub for damn near thirty-six years, Fin."

"So once again the fucking pub is going to take my da from me?" Fin got up and took his clothes off and sat down on the bed. "I'm going to take a shower. I'm so angry at this place right now I feel like burning it to the ground." Fin walked into the bathroom and shut the door.

Mick watched Fin disappear once again behind a closed door, but this time he wouldn't let him hide. Mick got up and took his jeans off.

He found Fin standing underneath the hot spray. He slid open the door and stood, asking Fin's permission to enter with his eyes. Fin looked at him for a moment then pulled him into his arms and shut the door.

"Need you, Mick. Hold me please." Fin had Mick wrapped up so tightly he could barely move his arms to hold him back. He managed to get his arms free and slipped them around Fin's neck. He pulled Fin's head down and gave him his heart and soul in a kiss. The longer they kissed the tighter the steel bands around his midsection became. Mick thought he honestly might pass out from lack of oxygen.

He broke the kiss. "Can't breathe. Too tight."

Fin loosened his grip. "Sorry, sweetheart. I just need you."

"You got me, baby." Mick ran his fingers lovingly through Fin's hair. "You've got me for as long as you want me."

Fin leaned down and took Mick's lips again. What started as a simple thank you kiss exploded into a torrent of passion, both of them touching and licking each other. Fin rubbed his burgeoning cock against Mick's. He moved from side to side and when his cock was fully erect he picked Mick up into his arms and wrapped Mick's legs around his waist. "Need you. Need to fuck you, sweetheart."

"Yes. Slick me quick with some shampoo."

Fin got the shampoo and held the cap in his mouth as he twisted the bottle. He spat the cap out of his mouth and squirted shampoo into Mick's hand. "You do it, Mick. I can't let you go."

Mick swiped the shampoo across his hole and ran his hand between their bodies and slicked Fin's eager cock. "Now. Do it now."

Fin lifted Mick a little higher and positioned his cock at Mick's opening. Mick slammed his ass down hard on Fin's cock. "Fuck."

He grabbed Fin's shoulders and hung on. He could tell Fin needed to do this on his own so he just held on and let Fin work his magic.

Fin's hips thrust back and forth, slamming Mick hard into the hard ceramic tiles. He was a man possessed. Mick kept his head down close to Fin's shoulder so the pounding of his body didn't lead to a concussion.

Fin's shouts as he came were a mixture of triumph and sorrow. Mick felt him release not only his cum but also his built-up stress. The look of utter love he received after Fin opened his eyes was enough to send him over the edge. The water quickly washed away the heat that spurted between them.

Fin didn't put Mick down, just got out of the shower and held him in one hand as he tried to dry them both with a warm towel. He carried Mick into the bedroom and crawled under the covers, still holding him tight.

Fin closed his eyes and kissed Mick's forehead. "Need to sleep. Just hold me until I wake up." And that quickly Fin was breathing deeply, fast asleep with Mick still wrapped around him.

Mick sighed and snuggled his head into Fin's neck and drifted off to sleep.

Chapter Six

The next morning Mick called around and found someone to come in and bartend for the day. He called Mel and asked her if she'd close up the pub after it closed. He told her to just leave the money in the safe in Sean's office because he didn't like having one of the women dropping off a bag full of money after midnight. He checked the stock behind the bar and swept and mopped, things he would normally have done the previous night but didn't. He opened the bar at eleven just like every day, but this wasn't a normal day.

Fin was still upstairs. He had asked if he could skip the pub thing. Mick had a feeling he was transferring his anger away from his da and to the pub instead. Mick didn't care. Whatever it took to get Fin through this he was willing to do.

He took care of the lunch crowd and at four o'clock Jesse came in to relieve him at the bar. He excused himself and went upstairs to see Fin. He found him on the couch watching one of his old high school football games. Although the look on his face told Mick he wasn't really seeing it. He got a couple cans of pop from the fridge and sat beside him on the couch.

He handed one of the cans to Fin and kissed him. "I've missed you today."

Fin opened the can and took a long drink. He set the can down and curled up on the couch with his head in Mick's lap. "Missed you too. I just couldn't go down there today."

Mick said nothing, just let Fin talk. He played with the silky black curls in his lap.

Fin turned back to the game awhile, lost in thought. "I don't know what to do or say to Da when I see him tomorrow night."

"That would depend on how you feel. Are you angry with Sean? If so you have to decide exactly what you're angry about. Is it that he didn't tell you earlier or that he wasn't the father you always wanted? Maybe you're even angry that he's going to die? Until you figure that out you won't know how to react when you see him."

Fin turned over onto his back so he could look up at Mick. "I think I've made my peace with the past. I'm not even mad at him for not telling me. Hell…I've been a lousy son since Mom died. The only thing I'm truly angry about is that I was thinking when he got back we could start over…you know? Start trying to build a father-son kind of relationship. Now I'm not going to get the chance."

Mick ran his fingers over Fin's facial features. "What kind of father-son relationship did you want to build with your da?"

Shrugging his shoulders, Fin captured Mick's hand and brought it to his lips. He kissed the fingers one by one, opened them and kissed Mick's palm. "Just the kind I've always dreamt about. The kind that other kids I grew up with had with their dads. I wanted him to take me fishing and maybe throw the football around in the park. You know…stupid stuff." He looked up at Mick and winked, giving him a devilish grin. "I want him to have to explain the facts of life and tell me to stay away from easy women."

Mick smacked him on the stomach. "Don't think that one's going to happen since he knows you're gay. The other things I think should still be doable though, the fishing for sure. We could take him back up the coast to my house and the two of you could fish the Atlantic if you wanted to."

Fin cocked his head to the side. "My da knows I'm gay?"

Mick smiled. "Yeah, your mother told him years ago, I guess. He told me one day by accident. He made me swear to never tell another living soul. I thought it was cute how protective he was of your privacy." Mick looked into Fin's eyes. "He never judged you for being who you are. Never."

Fin closed his eyes and lay there. Mick snuggled in to watch the rest of a game he'd already seen about seven times. It was the state championship game of Fin's senior year. Sean played the tape over and over during the past five summers.

Fin moved his head and Mick looked down. Fin was staring up into his eyes. "Can I tell him about us?"

Mick leaned down and kissed him. "I think he already must suspect, otherwise I don't think he would have asked me to tell you about his cancer. I'd just act naturally and let him bring it up if he feels comfortable doing so, but you do what you want. It's your decision." Mick lifted Fin's head so he could scoot down beside him on the couch.

They held each other and pretended to watch the game. "You know...I bet I've watched this game more than you have. It's one of Sean's favorites. Every summer when he starts missing you, this is one of the tapes he drags out of his stash. He makes everyone in the pub watch it. He even unplugs the jukebox." He ran his hands underneath Fin's t-shirt, just loving the feel of Fin's muscular chest under his fingers. He pinched and rubbed his nipples.

Fin pushed his leg between Mick's and rubbed Mick's cock with his knee. He pulled Mick down for a deep tongue-thrusting kiss. "Let's take our clothes off and watch the rest of the game in our skin."

Mick bounced up off the couch. "Sounds like a good plan but I'm going to get the lube just in case halftime comes early." Mick took off toward the bedroom, undressing on the way as Fin stood beside the couch and undressed.

In less than five minutes they were cuddled up back on the couch, this time skin to skin. Where last night Fin had needed it rough and fast, Mick could tell right now he needed to take it slow and easy. Fin was on his back and Mick was on his side against the back of the couch. He put his head down on Fin's chest, just petting his skin.

Fin's arms were wrapped around him softly stroking his back and butt. This was nice, thought Mick, sweet lazy love. He kissed Fin's chest and began to explore the entire wide muscled expanse with his lips and tongue. Fin groaned softly and ran his finger down Mick's crevice.

Latching on to one of Fin's nipples, Mick began to touch and play with Fin's sac. He felt the leathery smoothness of it. Though Fin didn't wax off his pubic hair like Mick did, he kept it trimmed nice and short. As Mick explored his cock visions began to pop into his head. "Have you ever thought of getting pierced down here somewhere?"

Chuckling, Fin pulled Mick up into his arms again. "Sure, I've thought about it. I could never get away with it sharing a locker room full of guys though. I just figured it would have to wait until after I retire." He kissed Mick's forehead. "Why? Have you thought about it?"

"Honestly, I've never even considered it…until now. Touching your cock just got me thinking about doing it for some reason. I don't know what I'd have done though. I'm kind of a baby when it comes to pain."

Fin ran his hand over Mick's cock. "Yeah, but you're my baby and I'm not sure I like the thought of some weird-looking dude with tattoos seeing this beautiful cock. Even if it is his job. I kind of like thinking it's only for me." Fin ran his hand up and down the length of Mick's erection. "Make love to me. I want to feel you in me."

Mick smiled and grabbed the lube. Fin had only let Mick fuck him a couple times so Mick was beyond ready. He squeezed a dollop of lube onto his fingers and began stretching Fin's tight puckered hole.

Groaning, Fin pushed into his fingers. "Oh God, Mick, that's enough. I need you in me."

Mick used what lube remained on his fingers to slick up his own cock. "How do you want it?" He rubbed his erection back and forth across Fin's opening.

"Hard, Mick. I need to feel you in me, hard and pounding." Fin put his legs over Mick's shoulders and opened himself up fully.

Positioning his cock, Mick leaned down and kissed him. "I love you, baby." With those words Mick pushed in hard and fast. He stilled for a minute to let Fin adjust to his size. When he felt Fin's muscles starting to relax he began a punishing rhythm of in and out. He pushed Fin across the couch with his hard strokes but Fin shoved back just as hard. When Fin's stomach muscles started to quiver Mick knew he was free to take his own pleasure. His hips pumped at a blinding speed until both men erupted at the same time. Fin painting his own chest with pearly drops of cum as Mick came deep inside Fin. They collapsed on the couch in a pile of arms and legs.

Mick rubbed Fin's back. After a while he said, "I'm going to go down and get us something for dinner. I think meatloaf was the special tonight, sound okay to you?"

Fin barely managed to open his eyes. "Sounds good but if I don't start working out I'm going to be too fat to run down the football field." He flashed Mick his signature smile and winked. "Although this new kind of exercising might be all I need…provided I get enough of it."

* * * * *

Friday morning Fin went to the local gym to work out and Mick made arrangements once again for a backup bartender. He gathered the staff and told them about Sean's health. He explained that Sean would be coming back into the country that day but he didn't know when he'd feel up to coming into the pub.

Mick also told them not to discuss Sean's health with Fin around. Although Mick wasn't sure how much Fin would actually be in the pub from now on. His anger toward the pub hadn't diminished in the slightest.

At five o'clock Fin walked through the door of the pub. Mick smiled, surprised to see him.

Fin walked up to the bar. "I was wondering if you'd like to go get a bite to eat before we pick up Da." Fin kinda squirmed on the barstool.

Mick knew Fin wanted to get out of the pub. He looked up at the clock. "Jesse should be here any minute then it'll just take me a second to run upstairs and change my shirt." Mick leaned on the bar in front of him and spoke softly. "I want to kiss you right now."

Fin actually blushed. "I wish you could, Mick. Why don't you go up and change while I watch the bar?"

"Are you sure about that?" Mick studied his reaction.

Fin came around the end of the bar. He threw a bar rag at Mick. "Get on with ya, lad. The sooner ye change the sooner we leave." Fin smiled and Mick nodded and headed up the stairs.

Jesse walked through the door a couple minutes later. "Hey, Fin. I heard your dad is comin' home today. I thought he'd be gone another couple weeks?" Jesse put his long blond hair back in a ponytail.

Fin didn't know if he should tell him the real reason his da was coming home. "Well, he's sick and his doctor thinks he should come back to the U.S. before he gets stuck over there."

Jesse looked up from wiping the bar down. "What do you mean sick?"

Putting his hands on his hips, Fin looked down. "He's got lung cancer. I guess he's had it awhile but Mick was the only one he told."

Fin watched as Jesse's jaw tightened with emotion. "Sorry to hear that. He's a great old man."

Nodding, Fin looked around the bar. "Yeah, this bar's been his whole life. Who'd have thought it would end up killin' him in the end." Fin walked toward the door. "Tell Mick I'll be waiting in the car."

Jesse nodded as Fin walked out the door. When Mick came downstairs Jesse relayed the message. "Fin said to tell you he'd be in the car." Jesse came around the end of the bar and leaned closer to Mick. "He told me about Sean. I take it Fin's blaming this place, huh?"

Mick nodded. "He's looking for something to blame right now. I'm just glad he's blaming the bar and not Sean or me." Mick started to walk off and stopped. Turning back to the bar, he looked at Jesse. "Do you think you'd be willing to go full-time for a while? I'd like to get Sean and Fin out of Boston later this week."

"Sure, I can work full-time until classes start again in the fall." Jesse put his hand on Mick's shoulder. "You can concentrate on taking care of the Finnegans."

Mick looked at Jesse stunned. Did Jesse know about him and Fin? They'd been so careful. "Why did you say it like that, Jes?"

Jesse shrugged his shoulders. "I'm not blind or judgmental. Those two are both going to need you in the coming months. Don't worry. I also don't gossip."

Mick slapped Jesse on the back. "Thanks, man. I'll see ya later."

Mick walked out the front door and looked for Fin's car. He didn't see the little sports car Fin had rented. A honk sounded and Mick looked at a large black SUV. Walking up to the car, Mick peered inside and saw Fin. He opened the door and got in. "What happened to your rental?"

Fin looked around the street then leaned over and kissed him. "I thought this would be better for Da so I traded them at the rental agency. The backseats fold down and together to form a bed."

Fin started the SUV and pulled away from the curb. "I hope I don't need that particular feature but I've got it just in case." Fin reached out and took Mick's hand. "So where would you like to eat dinner?"

* * * * *

They ate chili dogs and waffle fries at a little diner on the way to the airport. Fin was driving to the airport when Mick heard Fin's stomach start to rumble. Rubbing his midsection, he looked over at Mick. "Maybe the chili dogs weren't such a good idea."

Mick squeezed his hand. "We both know it's not the chili dogs that have your stomach upset. Try to relax. You still have plenty of time with Sean to make things right. I thought maybe we could take him to my beach house later this week. What do ya think?"

Fin continued to rub his stomach. "I think we'll have to see how Da feels. I'm not sure about him being so far away from his doctor right now."

Mick turned in his seat to look at Fin. "You know the doctor can't help him, don't you? The only thing that can be done for Sean is to make him comfortable until it's his time to go. He'll die at home. That's the way he wants it."

Fin pulled his hand out of Mick's and put it on the steering wheel. "Well, we don't always get what we want now, do we? If he thinks I'm gonna sit back and watch him die without doing something he's crazy…and so are you."

Mick rubbed his jaw. He hoped that after watching Sean suffer Fin'd understand Sean's wishes. "It's not an argument I'm willing to get into with you right now. I know you're mad at the world but I won't add more fuel to your fire."

Fin smacked the dashboard with his hand. "I'm just so fuckin' pissed. I wish I could punch something."

Mick shook his head. "Don't look at me. Maybe you should park the car and take a short run before Sean's plane comes in."

Fin breathed deeply and exhaled. "No, there isn't time. I'll take a good long run once we get Da back home." He pulled into the parking garage and turned off the ignition. "What'll we do about us? I want you with me. I need you with me right now."

Mick leaned over the console and kissed him. "Let's play that one by ear."

Chapter Seven

&

Mick waited outside the security gate as Fin paced back and forth along the corridor. He wished things were different and he could hold Fin in his arms and soothe the savage beast within him. People started coming through the arrival gate and Mick called to Fin.

Fin nodded his head and walked over to stand by him. "I'm not sure I'm ready yet."

Mick put his hand on Fin's shoulder. "No one is ever ready for this, baby. Just be honest with your da and you'll get through it."

Fin raised a brow. "In other words don't act happy if I'm not. Good advice but I'm used to putting on the mask of happiness with strangers."

Mick swallowed. There was a world of hurt in that one simple statement. Mick gave Fin's shoulder a squeeze and let go. He spotted Sean walking through the doorway. He looked gray. Not a good sign. He was also wheeling a small oxygen tank with tubes running around his head and to his nose. Mick closed his eyes. His throat started to close up and his eyes began to burn. He wasn't ready to let his old friend go. He swallowed and blinked his eyes several times, trying to dry the tears that had begun to form.

He stepped toward Sean and embraced his dear friend. "Good to have you home, Sean." He held on another few seconds then stepped back.

Fin stepped forward and stuck out his hand. Sean looked at the hand and frowned. He shook Fin's hand. "Good to have you back, Da."

"Thank you, Calder." Sean looked around the terminal. "I need to sit down for a minute until the bags start arriving." He walked over to a row of chairs and sat down. Mick looked at Fin. "Why don't you go wait for his bags and I'll go sit with him." Fin nodded and Mick took his wrist and brought him close. "I love you."

Fin cleared his throat and nodded. "Me too. I'll get the bags. They shouldn't be too hard to spot as long as those damn shamrock stickers are still stuck all over them." Fin walked off toward the baggage claim and Mick went over and sat down beside Sean.

"How're you feeling, Sean? Was the plane ride too rough on you?" Mick put his arm around the back of Sean's chair.

"Yeah, it was pretty rough. I guess I should've never gone in the first place. I just thought I'd have more time." Sean pounded his fist against his thigh. "Damn it, they said I'd have more time." He looked over at Mick. "What am I going to do about Calder?"

Mick took Sean's fist in his hands. "You're going to become the father you've always wanted to be without worrying about the pub. That's my problem now."

Sean nodded his head. "Thank you, but I'm not sure if Calder will let me in. I've wasted too much time already."

"He'll let you in. He wants you to go fishing. I guess it's something he always wanted to do with you when he was growing up. I don't care if I have to wheel you out to the shore myself but you will go fishing with your son before you die."

Sean raised an eyebrow. "Sounds like you've gotten to know my son pretty well, Mick. Is there something you'd like to tell me?"

Mick cleared his throat and looked Sean in the eye. "Not much to tell. I love him, he knows it and loves me back but his career comes first. He'll be gone in another couple of weeks and I'll be alone again. In the meantime he's mine and I'll see to it that you do right by him."

Sean patted Mick's thigh. "I knew you would. He'll have no one after I'm gone. I know my son well enough to know he'll try to push you away when the hurt becomes too much. It'll be up to you to fight for him. He's good at shutting himself off, believe me, and if you let him that's exactly what he'll do." He looked Mick in the eye. "Just how fast are you, Mick? Fast enough to keep a running back from running?"

Mick didn't get a chance to answer before Fin was rolling two suitcases toward them. He stopped in front of them and looked at Sean. "I'll get the car and bring it to the curb."

Mick nodded and Fin wheeled the suitcases toward the exit. "I hope I'm fast enough, Sean, because I can't imagine my life without him."

* * * * *

The next few days were spent in either the doctors' building or the hospital having more tests run on Sean. The oncologist tried to determine how much longer Sean had to live. The cancer had spread massively in the past month and the doctor told Sean it was time to get his affairs in order. They expected him to live another one to two months at best. As predicted Fin argued with the doctor and demanded a second opinion.

The doctor took him aside and discussed the extent of the invasive cancer in Sean's body. Fin quietly nodded his head and turned back toward Sean. "Let's go home, Da."

They got back to the house and Sean went upstairs to rest. Fin watched him struggle with the stairs and turned to Mick. "We need to order him a hospital bed and have it put in the study. It's already gettin' too hard for him to get up the stairs." He strode toward the phone and placed a call to the insurance company to inquire about a bed. When he got off the phone he turned toward Mick. "They'll have someone call back. They asked me if hospice had been called. Do you think we really need to invite outsiders into this?"

Mick walked over and pulled Fin into his arms. "Yeah, baby, I do. When it gets down to the end they'll help Sean manage his pain and they'll help you deal with it."

"I don't want to see him in pain. If they can help him with that I'll understand the need for them but they won't be able to help me deal with it." He kissed Mick. "I love you but I have to tell you that I'm not sure even you'll be able to help me deal with it. I'll need to do things my own way, it's just the way I am."

Mick led him over to the couch and pulled him into a tight embrace. "Let's think about now. What would you like to do with Sean first?"

"I'd like to talk to him. Try to understand why he did the things he did. Most of the things I've dreamt about involve more physical activity than Da is up to. I'd like to watch a football game with him and fish. Other than that I wonder if he'd be up for a friendly game of poker." Fin shrugged his shoulders. "I just wanna get to know him, I guess."

Mick kissed Fin's cheek. "You can do all those and more but you have to be willing to listen and not judge. Sean needs this as much as you do so you have to ask yourself…what gift you are willing to give him before he dies."

Fin looked at Mick through narrowed eyes. "What's that supposed to mean?" He started to sit up but Mick pulled him back into his arms.

"It means that Sean wants to become the father you've always wanted. He knows that he's screwed up in the past but he wants a relationship with you man to man…father to son." When Fin just stared at him Mick could feel his own temper surfacing.

"Look, Fin, you've got a chance here that a lot of people including myself don't get. You've the chance to set things right with your dad before he dies. If you don't take full advantage of the time Sean has left you're a fool. Do you know what I'd give to have just one hour with my mom back? Just one hour to tell her how sorry I am for the way I treated her in the end."

Mick took a deep breath. "Listen to me. When he dies it's too late. All I'm asking is that you try to put away the bitterness and accept the gift of time. I love you and I'll be with you every step of the way. Pour your frustrations out to me if you need to but make peace with Sean while you have the chance."

Fin closed his eyes and embraced Mick tighter. Pulling him onto his lap, Fin kissed him. "I understand what you're saying. I'm not sure how it's going to work but I'll try as long as you're with me." He kissed Mick again and allowed his lips to travel down the long corded column of Mick's neck. He pulled Mick's shirt up so he could touch more skin.

Mick arched his back and ran his fingers through Fin's hair. "That feels good, keep goin'."

Fin smiled and flipped Mick down on the couch. He knelt beside him and started working on his jeans. "Wanna taste you, sweetheart." Fin started at Mick's lips and worked his way down stopping to give the dark brown nipples the attention they deserved. He followed the line of hair down to Mick's groin and buried his nose there.

Mick moaned and raised his knees, planting his feet on the couch. "Love me, baby."

Fin looked up into Mick's eyes and smiled. "Always." He took the heavy erection in front of his face and licked from base to crown. Fin paid special attention to the sensitive area just under the head and sucked gently. Sliding the erection into his mouth, he moaned. God, Mick tasted good. He felt each vein with his tongue, hollowing his cheeks as he sucked more of him in. Sliding his mouth up and down the pulsing cock, Fin reached down and unzipped his own jeans. Taking his erection in hand, he started pumping his cock with the rhythm of his mouth.

Mick pulled his legs up even higher. "I wanna taste you too, baby."

Fin released Mick's cock and took off his jeans. He straddled Mick's head on the couch and went back to work on Mick's cock as Mick enveloped his needy erection into his own hot mouth. Fin thrust his cock gently into Mick's willing mouth as he continued to devour Mick's shaft.

Mick moaned and thrust upward. "Gonna come." He thrust up a few more times and Fin swallowed him as deep as he could as Mick came. The sensations were so perfectly erotic that Fin let loose his own stream of cum down Mick's willing throat.

Fin tried his best not to collapse on Mick but he only managed to get his feet on the floor before his head fell to Mick's thighs. He was half on and half off the couch when they heard movement upstairs. Fin jumped up and looked for his jeans. They dressed quickly and Fin went to the bathroom to wash up while Mick found a can of air freshener. The smell of sex was quickly covered by the smell of potpourri just as Sean headed down the stairs.

Fin came back into the room as Sean entered. "Would you like some supper now, Da?" Fin sat down on the couch next to Mick.

Sean sat in his usual faded green recliner. "I'm not hungry but thank you, Calder, for asking. I'm just going to watch a little television and then maybe I'll feel hungry."

Fin looked at Mick and shrugged. "Hey, Da, can I ask you a question?" At Sean's nod Fin continued. "Why do you still call me Calder when the rest of the world calls me Fin?"

Sean closed his eyes and leaned back in the chair. "To keep the name alive, I guess. Didn't your mom tell you where you got your name?"

Fin leaned forward on the couch leaning on his knees. "No, she didn't. I guess she thought you'd tell me."

Sean opened his eyes and looked at his son. "When I was a boy back in Ireland my best friend's name was Calder. One day the two of us went ice fishing and Calder fell through a thin patch of ice. I tried everything I could to get him out. Finally I ran for help but by the time it arrived it was too late for him. I made a promise to him right then and there that if I ever had a son I would name him Calder. Fin's a good name but I named you Calder for a reason."

Fin nodded his head. "I wish you'd told me that story before, Da."

Sean looked out the window beside his chair. "There's a lot of things I should've told you earlier, son." Sean looked at Mick. "Who's running the pub while you're spending so much time away?"

Mick smiled and rubbed Fin's back absentmindedly. "Jesse Farrell's taking over for a couple weeks but I have to work tomorrow night. Saturdays are just too busy not to. Would you like to go in for a while? A lot of people have been asking for you."

Sean looked at Fin. "Only if Calder will go with me and have a Guinness with his old man."

Fin shook his head. "How can you stand to go into the place that gave you cancer? I'd think you'd never want set foot in that place again." Fin could feel the heat creeping up his face.

Tilting his head, Sean looked confused. "The pub didn't do this to me, son. Life did this to me. People get cancer. If not cancer then something else kills 'em. I don't have the time to place blame and you shouldn't either. The people in that pub are like family. Especially since your mom died. I'd just like a chance to finally have a beer with my son. If you don't want to just say so."

Fin ran his fingers through his hair. He didn't know what to think anymore. The things Mick said to him replayed through his mind. "Okay, Da. I'd like to have a beer with you.

We'll go in for a while tomorrow night and listen to the band and have a Guinness." Fin got up and walked toward the kitchen. "I'm going to make soup and sandwiches if anyone's interested."

Mick watched him leave. "I'll be in shortly." Fin nodded and disappeared through the door. Mick looked at Sean. "He's diverting his anger to the pub as you can tell. I figured it was better the pub than either of us. I'm glad you talked him into having a beer though." He got up from the couch and headed toward the kitchen. He turned back toward Sean. "One step at a time, Sean."

* * * * *

Fin drove his da to the pub the next evening. The band was slated to start at eight. Fin looked at the clock on the dash. They had forty-five minutes to get something to eat before the music started. Fin hoped he could open up and talk to his da after a few beers. He'd tried all day to gather his courage.

He knew he loved his da. He felt it in every regret and every tear. Now he was going to do his best to like his da. "Mick says the band is a good one. Hopefully he saved us a table."

Sean chuckled. "If I know Mick he's saving us a place at the bar. I don't think he wants either of us too far away from him right now." Sean turned in his seat to look at Fin. "He loves you. You know that, right?"

Fin kept his eyes on the road. "Yeah, I know. I feel the same way but it doesn't bode well for my football career." Fin tried to swallow the lump in his throat. "I'll have to let him go when I leave Boston. It wouldn't be fair to him to wait for the two years left on my contract."

Sean narrowed his eyes. "Who says you can't have both? Is there a new rule in the football league that I don't know about?"

Tightening his hands on the wheel, Fin glanced over at his da. "No rule except the good old boy rule. You know what it'd be like for a professional athlete to come out of the closet?"

Sean merely nodded his head. "Hard, I imagine. I guess it would just depend on how much you wanted both." Sean turned his head to look out the window. "Why don't you tell Mick to bring a bag over to the house? There's no reason the two of you shouldn't be together while you can."

Fin's jaw dropped. Luckily they were pulling up to the pub. "You don't mind us sleeping together under your roof?"

"Why would I mind, son? I like it that the two people I love most are together. I've spent far too long in a pub to be judgmental." Sean opened his door and got out.

Fin opened his door and raced around the SUV to open the pub door for his da. They walked in to a very noisy crowd. When the patrons turned to see Sean they all gave their greetings. It seemed most of the people in attendance knew Sean.

Fin watched his da shake hands with people as he walked toward the bar. Mick raised his hand to get Fin's attention. Pointing toward the end of the bar, Mick flashed Fin his dimples. He still didn't know how he'd gotten lucky enough to have Mick, but he planned on enjoying every second of it. He sat on the designated stool and waited for Mick to finish a drink order.

Mick strode toward Fin, all smiles. When he got closer he leaned forward. "Glad to see you both made it." Mick looked over at a laughing Sean. "He's happy here. Can you see it?"

Fin looked over his shoulder at his da. "Yeah, I see it." He turned back toward Mick. "Are you going to sing for me tonight, sweetheart?"

"I'll sing whatever you want, baby." Mick left to build a Guinness for each of them.

When he set them down on the bar in front of Fin he grinned. "I especially like to sing in the shower." He wagged his eyebrows.

Fin laughed. He realized it was the first time he'd laughed in several days. "Da says you should bring a bag over and stay with us. I mean…stay with me."

"Really? That's good because I'm not gettin' near enough love from you lately." Mick looked over at Sean. "Jeff cooked Sean's favorite today, do you think he's up to eating tonight?"

Fin shrugged, his da hadn't been eating much of anything since he'd been back from Ireland. "It depends on what his favorite is, I guess."

Mick put his hand on Fin's shoulder. He could tell it bothered Fin that he didn't even know his dad's favorite food. "He's Irish. His favorite is corned beef and cabbage with a side of fried potatoes."

Fin rubbed his forehead. "I don't think the cabbage would be good for his stomach right now but the rest sounds bland enough he might feel like it." As Fin finished Sean sat down on the stool next to him.

"I might feel like what?" Sean asked, looking from Fin to Mick.

Mick pushed the beer toward Sean. "Jeff made you some corned beef and cabbage today. Can I get you a plate?"

Fin could tell by the look on Sean's face that he didn't want anything but he didn't want to hurt Jeff's feelings. "Maybe a little bit of the corned beef. My stomach isn't feeling up to much else."

Mick nodded and looked at Fin. "What about you?"

"I'll have a couple chicken strips and some of the fried potatoes but let me get it. You've got enough to deal with and I know my way around the kitchen." Fin got up from his stool and headed for the kitchen.

Mick watched him go then turned back to Sean. "Tell me how you're feeling…and be honest."

Looking down into his Guinness, Sean sighed. "It's getting harder to breathe every hour. I feel like my lungs are filling up with cotton but I'm determined to finish what I started with Calder. So don't let on to him."

Filling another drink order, Mick thought about keeping one more thing from Fin. He shook his head. "No, damn it." He'd talk to Fin when they got home. He wouldn't keep anything else from him. Mick finished the order and went back to where Fin and Sean were now eating their dinner. "How 'bout we go fishing Sunday? I thought we could drive up the coast and spend the day, maybe come back Monday afternoon."

Fin looked at Sean. "Do you feel up to fishing, Da? Mick's got a terrific house overlooking the Atlantic."

Sean grinned. "Just stick me in the car and take me wherever you want to go. I have to warn you though. I haven't fished since I was a teenager."

* * * * *

The night was a success as far as Fin was concerned. They listened to the music and managed to talk in between sets. Sean told him all about his grandparents who'd brought him to Boston from Ireland when he was still a boy. His da told him stories of his trip to Ireland and made Fin promise to visit the country of his ancestors someday.

The highlight of the night for both of them was hearing Mick sing. He sang six songs that night. Two of the songs were love ballads and Fin caught Mick looking at him several times during the songs. Sean's eyes pooled with tears when Mick sang his rendition of "Danny Boy", his da's favorite.

Driving home, Sean fell asleep before Fin even made it to the end of the street. He drove home feeling hopeful. He pulled up to the house and got his da into bed. Sean surprised him by asking Fin to hook up his oxygen tank. Fin did as his da asked then went to sit in front of the TV and wait for Mick to get home.

* * * * *

At almost three o'clock Mick came through the door. He set his bag down and locked the front door before noticing Fin asleep on the couch. Mick's heart melted at the sight before him. Fin had obviously tried his best to stay awake for him. His head was slumped forward with his chin on his chest. Ouch, that was going to hurt tomorrow.

Mick walked over to the couch and put his hand on the back of Fin's head. "Baby, it's time for bed." He smiled to himself when Fin jumped up off the couch and spun toward him.

"Sorry. I tried to stay awake for you." He leaned in and kissed Mick. "It was a good night, wasn't it?"

Mick smiled and pulled Fin into his arms. "It was a great night. I think Sean knew it might be the last time he got to go to the pub. I'm glad he enjoyed himself."

Fin led Mick toward the stairs. "He asked me to hook up his oxygen for him tonight. I think we should stop by his room and make sure he's okay before going to bed."

Fin kept walking up the stairs but Mick could tell it was really bothering him. They checked on Sean and quietly closed his bedroom door. He pulled Fin into his bedroom and kissed him. "He didn't want you to know but he told me it's getting harder to breathe by the hour. I think from now on we should insist he wear the oxygen whenever possible. The only reason he isn't wearing it all the time now is because he doesn't want you to know how bad he's feeling."

Fin pulled off Mick's shirt and then his own. "Get into bed with me, sweetheart. I need you to hold me." Fin finished undressing and crawled into bed.

Mick pulled off his jeans and underwear and crawled in beside him. He ran his fingers over Fin's beautiful face and kissed him. "Have you talked to anyone in New York about taking some family leave if you need to?"

Fin shook his head. "No. I talked to my agent and told him I couldn't leave until Da passed but I haven't talked to anyone from the team. It's only May so I thought I'd see how things went until the end of the month. I think as long as I continue training on my own they'll be fine." Fin kissed him again. "Enough talkin', more fuckin'." He gave Mick that devilish grin he loved.

Mick rolled his eyes and straddled Fin's hips. "You have such a way with words." He bent over and traced Fin's lips with his tongue dipping in for small tastes as his hands roamed down Fin's chest. He rubbed the well-developed muscles as he made love to Fin's mouth.

Groaning, Fin grabbed Mick's hair and deepened the kiss. He explored his mouth with his tongue while grinding his cock against Mick's. He pulled back from the kiss and ran his hands down the leanly muscled chest. "God, you're sexy. Do you have any idea how much I need this right now? Just the feel of your hands on me is about to make me explode."

Mick spread his thighs farther apart and Fin took quick advantage. He started at Mick's mouth and worked his way down. Licking and chewing on the soft flesh, Fin stopped to pay his respects to Mick's hardened nipples before moving down to lick and nibble at his amazing cock.

Sliding his tongue around the crown, Fin groaned. "Good…so good." He lifted Mick's sac and licked his way around the tender flesh, sucking one orb at a time into his mouth.

Mick needed more because he reached down and hooked his arms under his knees and pulled them to his chest, exposing the puckered hole that Fin loved so much. "Eat me…want it, baby."

Fin rimmed Mick with his tongue, taking long swipes and then little swirling jabs. He gently scraped the tender area with his teeth. Mick must've enjoyed his playing because he began to moan and rock toward Fin's face. Fin continued with his quest to drive Mick out of his mind. A bottle of lube suddenly appeared before his eyes.

"Fuck me, baby." Mick looked down into his eyes.

Nodding, he took the bottle of lube and drizzled a bit around Mick's hole. Taking his time to rub and prepare his lover, Fin felt an overwhelming sense of love. "Love you."

Mick grabbed his arms and hauled him upward. He took his mouth like a man on a mission. "Now. I need you now." He hooked his legs over Fin's shoulders.

Fin kissed him once more before lining up and pushing deep inside. Mick groaned at the pleasure-pain of the driving force behind the thrust. "*Oh fuck!*"

Fin grinned down at Mick and put his finger to his lips. "Get ready." He set up a fast driving pace in and out of Mick's ass. The muscles of Mick's chest heaved and bunched at the onslaught of Fin's passion.

Moaning and thrashing his head back and forth on the pillow, Mick grabbed his cock, feeling his balls draw up. "Gonna…" Fin continued, bending occasionally to kiss him. "Close…so close."

Two more tugs on his cock and Mick erupted onto his own chest. The squeeze of his muscles pushed Fin over the edge.

With his whole body shaking and trembling in ecstasy Fin collapsed on top of him. "So good. Always so good."

Mick wrapped his arms around Fin. "Mine."

Fin nodded and burrowed into his neck. "Yours."

Chapter Eight

❧

"I got one!" Fin shouted as he struggled to reel the fish in. He looked over at Sean who was sitting in a chair next to the water with his own pole.

Mick ran up behind him laughing. "Sure you can get it in by yourself?"

Grinning, Fin winked. "I can get it in just fine, smarty pants." He continued to struggle with the fish as Sean gave him directions. When the fish was close enough to shore, Mick swooped in and scooped the fish into a net.

Laughing his ass off, Mick brought the net to Fin. "I'm glad you didn't catch a grown-up fish. As much trouble as this little baby one gave you, I can't imagine what you would have done with a legal-sized fish."

Peering into the net, Fin's jaw dropped. The damn fish was only about five inches long. It looked more like a piece of bait than a fish. He looked back up at Mick. "No way could that tiny fish be the one I reeled in. You must have switched them."

Wiping tears from his eyes, Mick laughed. "Sorry, baby. No switching."

Fin was feeling let down until a hand on his shoulder had him turning. His da was standing beside him with a smile on his face. "It's a nice fish." He looked up at Fin. "You should be proud, son. It's a good day when a man catches his first fish. After all, it's not the fish but the catching that's the fun." He patted Fin's shoulder. "Let's get it out of the net and take a picture before the poor fella dies."

Mick handed Fin the net and ran back to their gear to grab the camera while Fin tried to untangle the fish from the net. He was afraid the fish might be a goner at this point but at least he'd get a picture.

Coming back with the camera, Mick aimed it at him and Sean. "Hold up the fish by the line so we can see how big it is. Or isn't," he chuckled.

Fin felt his da's hand settle more firmly on his shoulder as he held up the fish. He knew he'd cherish this picture for the rest of his life. After Mick snapped the picture he quickly came over and took the fish from Fin.

He watched him as he carefully pulled out the hook and lowered the fish into the ocean. Giving it a few good swirls in the water, he released it. Fin couldn't tell if the fish was alive or dead at that point and he had a feeling Mick would never tell him the truth about it anyway.

Feeling truly happy for the first time in several days, Fin put his arm around his da. "Thanks for teaching me how to fish."

Sean looked at Fin with misty eyes. "It was one of the greatest joys of my life." He elbowed Fin in the side and gestured toward Mick. "Don't let that scallywag fool you. He's just as proud of you for catching that fish as I am."

Fin noticed the last of his da's statements was softer, more out of breath. "Are you ready to go back to the house?" At his da's nod, Fin looked over at Mick. "I'm going to take Da back to the house. Are you okay carrying the gear and his chair?"

Mick smiled and flexed his lean muscles. "Don't worry about me. I'd carry the world for you."

Fin knew Mick spoke the truth. He felt a lump form in his throat just as his da started coughing. Shaking his head once, Fin turned and picked his da up in his arms. Making his way to the steep man-made staircase built into the side of the bluff, Fin prayed he still had a little more time.

Sean had to rest the next couple of days so they just stayed in and played poker and watched movies. Thursday night they all took in a baseball game. Mick managed to get tickets on the lowest level of the stadium so Da didn't have to do a lot of climbing. He and Mick ate park food until they both felt sick, but Da wasn't eating much these days. He'd even taken to carrying the portable oxygen tank on his back whenever they left the house.

Fin knew time was getting short, so he spent as much time as possible with his da. He smiled when he thought of his da trying to teach him how to split and shuffle cards with one hand. Evidently his da had picked up more than just bartending skills at the pub. Every time Fin tried to manipulate the cards they ended up all over the floor. His hands were just too damn big for card tricks, he finally told his da. His da just smiled and told him not to quit his day job. Fin opened the car door with a smile still on his face.

Mick had something special planned tonight, he'd said. It was Saturday and Fin knew Mick would have to work at the pub so he couldn't figure out what he'd planned. He entered the kitchen, whistling, only to find Mick hard at work at the stove. He walked up and wrapped his arms around him. "Hey, sweetheart, what ya cooking?"

Leaning back into his chest, Mick turned his head to kiss him. "Chicken fried steak and mashed potatoes for you and Sean to eat for dinner."

Fin kissed Mick's neck. "More like chicken fried steak for me and mashed potatoes for Da."

"Where've you been? I got home and couldn't find you." Mick put the top on the pan of potatoes and turned into Fin's embrace.

"Da asked me to get him some candy orange slices and stuff. I just got back." Fin ran his hands down Mick's back to his oh-so-tempting ass and pulled him away from the stove.

Mick pulled back a little and looked Fin in the eye. "You know the doctor said no more candy for him."

Shrugging his shoulders, Fin kissed the top of Mick's nose. "So? The man's dying, with or without candy. Let him have what makes him happy."

"And what do you plan to do about his diabetes? Are you trying to hurry the process up so you can get the hell out of here? Is that it?" As soon as the words were out of his mouth Fin could see the regret in Mick's eyes but the damage had already been done.

Fin pulled completely away and walked out of the kitchen. "Fuck you." Fin went immediately to his room and changed into his workout gear. He needed to get out of the house before Mick came back to apologize. He knew Mick didn't mean what he'd said but he was barely holding on to his emotions as it was and the last thing he needed was a confrontation with his lover.

Running down the stairs, he spotted Mick coming out of the kitchen toward him. "Drop it. I'm going for a run." He heard Mick start to protest but he blocked him out and dashed out the front door.

He ran down the streets of Boston to the park. Setting up a punishing pace, Fin ran away from his troubles. By the time he'd run a grueling twelve miles and made his way back to the house he was no longer mad at Mick, though the hurt remained.

Walking into the house, he made his way straight to the shower. He stripped off his clothes and turned the water on hot. Stepping in, Fin let the water relieve his tired muscles. He was going to have to start working out more so he'd be ready for the season. He was probably already in deep shit with the team trainer for skipping out on preseason training but some things were more important.

After washing up, Fin turned off the water and opened the shower door to find Mick leaning against the sink. Mick could barely look him in the eye. "Sorry. I'm an ass."

Fin simply nodded and walked toward him. "You are. But I love you anyway."

Mick opened his arms and he walked right into them. Kissing his face, Mick continued to apologize. "I know you love your da. I love him too. I don't have a good excuse as to why I got all pissy about the candy other than I know you'll leave me soon." He kissed Fin's throat.

Fin held Mick even tighter. "I honestly think my da is gonna go fast. When a dying man asks for candy you get it for him." He rubbed his nude half-hard cock against the front of Mick's soft faded jeans. "What time do you have to leave for the pub?"

Mick took a quick bite of Fin's neck. "In another fifteen minutes. The food's in the oven keeping warm. I brought home the data projection unit from the club and put it up in Sean's room. I thought the two of you could watch one of your games tonight. I brought home a couple of Sean's favorites."

Damn, that made Fin like a complete shit. Mick had gone to a lot of trouble to make a memory for him and he'd gone ape shit over one little comment that he knew Mick didn't even mean.

Kissing his way around Mick's face, Fin stopped to dip his tongue into the recesses of Mick's hot mouth. "Thanks for the dinner and the films. What time will you be home tonight? I need to thank you properly for everything you've done for me and Da."

Mick ran his hand down the crease of Fin's naked ass. "Not until around two-thirty. Don't wait up for me. I'll be sure and wake you when I get into bed."

Stepping back, Fin looked down at Mick. "Sorry, sweetheart, it looks like I got you all wet."

Mick looked down at himself and laughed. "Wet is one thing, it will dry, but the cum tracks across the front of my jeans you left might get me a few odd looks." He kissed Fin once more and headed for the closet. Pulling out a dark blue polo shirt and another pair of faded jeans, Mick redressed.

Fin sat on the bed totally naked and watched Mick as he stroked his throbbing cock. Mick raised an eyebrow and went to kneel in front of Fin.

"Is someone looking for some quick relief before I go?" He leaned forward and swiped the length of Fin's cock with his tongue.

"Don't stop." Fin fell back on the bed and spread his thighs. He reached down and ran his fingers through Mick's hair as Mick gave his cock a thorough tongue bath. "So good." Fin began to thrust into Mick's mouth.

Holding his head still, Mick allowed Fin to fuck his mouth. When he pulled up and off his cock to travel down to Fin's sac, Fin groaned. "Oh yeah. Just like that." One at a time, Mick sucked his balls into his mouth while his finger started pushed against Fin's hole. When he breached his hole with not one but two fingers, Fin almost vibrated off the bed. "Shit, that feels good."

Releasing Fin's balls, Mick traveled back up the length of his engorged cock. He scraped the tender skin with his teeth as Fin continued to moan. "Gonna come," Fin declared as Mick slipped his lips over the crown of his shaft.

Mick continued to pump his fingers into Fin's ass as he hummed the national anthem around his cock. The vibrations sent Fin over the edge, cum shooting down Mick's throat.

"Fuck, Mick."

Mick licked him clean and stood. He looked down at his cum-soaked jeans. "Damn. I do twice as much laundry since I met you." He headed back over to the closet to change his jeans once again.

Fin smiled as he watched Mick pick up a dirty t-shirt off the floor and clean himself before putting on the fresh pair of jeans. When he walked back toward the bed with those dimples on display, Fin groaned and reached down to brush his hand across his still semi-hard cock. Leaning over the bed, he kissed Fin one last time. "That should hold you until I get home." He started to walk out the door.

"Don't flirt tonight, sweetheart. Remember you're mine." Fin was raised up on his elbows, smiling at him.

Smiling back, Mick winked. "Flirting gets me more tips but you're the only one allowed to get the real thing, baby. I don't want anyone else." He opened the door and looked back over his shoulder. "Ever."

* * * * *

Pulling up the hospital tray that came with Da's bed, Fin set the plate of mashed potatoes and a cup of chocolate pudding before him. "There's chicken fried steak too, Da, but I figured you weren't up to it." Fin came back into the room with his own dinner and set it on the TV tray beside his da's bed.

Sean was poking at his mashed potatoes. He'd taken his oxygen tube out to eat and Fin could see his chest laboring to get a breath. His jaws tightened at the sight before him, his once-strong da was wasting away before his eyes. His complexion was a dull shade of gray and his eyes had lost their spark. Fin knew it was time to call in hospice to help manage his da's pain. Sean never complained, never seemed to be angry at the situation but he could see the sadness in his eyes.

Fin finished his dinner and stood with his plate. He looked at Sean's still-full plate and then at his da. "You done, Da?"

Sean nodded and hooked the oxygen back under his nose. "Thanks, Calder. I'm just not hungry."

Fin nodded and took both plates into the kitchen. He rinsed them and put them into the dishwasher and got out the candy sack. He filled two small bowls, one with the candy orange slices and one with peanut butter clusters, then carried both bowls back into the study that he and Mick had converted into Sean's bedroom, Fin set the bowls on the hospital tray. "I got the candy you were askin' for."

He sat down on the edge of the hospital bed. "Mick thought maybe we'd like to watch one of my games tonight. Are you up for it?"

Sean reached for his hand. Swallowing the lump in his throat, Fin closed his eyes and took his da's hand.

"I'd like to watch your last All-American college game." Sean struggled to sit up. "I was so proud of you, Calder. I shut the pub down that day and invited all my regulars in for a big party to watch you play."

Fin could feel his eyes burning and his throat closing up. "Why didn't you ever come see me play in person, Da? You know I'd have flown you anywhere if you'd wanted to see me play."

Sean leaned back onto his pillow and turned his face away. "I didn't feel like I deserved it. I can't explain why I did the things I did when you were younger, Calder. By the time you made it to college ball I knew what I'd given up to make the pub a success and I felt like the worst father in the world. It's funny how you always think there'll be time, but once I had it we were like strangers. I knew it was my fault so I was never angry at anyone but myself for it."

Sean reached over and took a tissue out of the box by his bed. It was only then that Fin noticed the tears falling down his da's face. "I wish you'd called me sometimes, Da. I always felt like I was a disappointment or a burden to you. It's why I played football in the first place…to get your attention."

Sean wiped his face and turned his head toward him. "A disappointment? Didn't you know I've been proud of you every day of your life?" Sean's tears became a coughing fit.

Fin jumped up and hit his da on the back and turned up his oxygen flow. "It's okay, let's not talk about it any more."

Damn, why had he started this discussion? He knew it would upset them both.

Sean stopped coughing. "I've done more damage to you than I ever dared to imagine, haven't I?" He took the oxygen from his nose and blew his nose into the tissue. "Your mom tried to tell me so many times but I thought she was just overreacting. She was always so protective of you."

Fin knew this might be his only chance to understand why his mom stayed with his absent da. Even though he hated to upset him even more, Fin still needed a few answers. "I never understood why Mom kept defending you to me. She'd find me in my bedroom when I was feeling down about you missing yet another game and she always told me what a good father I had and how much he loved his family." Now it was Fin's turn to wipe at his eyes. "I just never understood why she loved you so much, I guess. You never seemed to be there for her just like you were never there for me. I remember getting angry with her for defending you."

Sean wiped his eyes again. "I loved your mom to the depths of my soul. It's different with a lover than a child. You had to go to bed most nights before I came home from the pub. But I slept with your mom every night. I held her in my arms and told her about my day as we made love. She'd tell me everything that went on here at home. All the cute things you'd done or said that day. She did such a good job of filling me in on your daily life that I didn't realize I was never here. And then one day, your mom was gone and suddenly I didn't have anyone to tell me about my own son. It was then that I realized I'd never formed the bond that dads usually have with their children. I know I didn't do right by you or her but I always made sure she knew she was my girl. I'm sorry I didn't take the time to make you feel the same way."

Fin didn't want to talk about this any more. He stood and went over to the box of tapes Mick had brought home from the office. He found the Rose Bowl game and put it in. "Let's just watch the game."

Sean nodded. "Would you sit up here on the bed with me so we can discuss the plays and stuff? I've always wondered what your thought process was during a game."

"Sure, Da. I'll just move the tray to the side. That way we can still both reach the candy bowls."

For the next two hours Fin discussed strategy and plays with his da. He was surprised to find out how much his da knew about football. By the time the game was over Sean had long since fallen asleep. After the tape finished Fin shut off the player and turned out the lights.

* * * * *

Walking into the kitchen with the still-full candy bowls, Fin looked at the clock. It was only ten-thirty. He decided to change his clothes and visit Mick at work for a few minutes.

Changing into his favorite worn and holey pair of jeans, Fin smiled and purposely left his underwear off. He grabbed the black silk-blend t-shirt out of the closet because it was Mick's favorite. Mick told him it showed his muscular chest off to perfection. Five minutes later he was driving toward the pub with a small tube of lube in his pocket.

Opening the door, he was hit with a blast of smoke. No wonder Da had lung cancer. He walked through the door and was met by shouts of hello from the regular patrons of the pub. Mick looked up and Fin could see the worried expression on his face from across the bar. Fin wasted no time getting to him to reassure him everything was all right. Before Mick could speak Fin held up his hand. "Da's fine. I left him sleeping and decided to stop in for a few minutes."

He could see the relief settle over Mick's glorious face. "How'd it go tonight?"

Fin shrugged his shoulders. "Good 'n bad. I'll talk to you later about it. How's your night been?"

Mick could tell that Fin was hurting. It was there in the worry lines around his eyes, red puffy eyes. Yep, Fin had definitely been crying. He motioned Jesse over and told him he was gonna take a quick break.

Coming around the end of the bar, Mick motioned upstairs. "Let's go up for a few minutes." Fin nodded and followed him to the loft apartment.

Mick pulled him over to the couch and sat Fin down and straddled his lap. "Did you wear these sexy-ass jeans and this tight shirt for me, baby?" He licked up the side of Fin's face and nibbled on his earlobe.

Fin wrapped his arms around him and squeezed. "For no one else that's for sure." He kissed Mick slow and sweet. "Sorry to pull you away from work but I needed to get out of the house for a while."

Mick nodded. "What happened?"

Burying his head in Mick's shoulder, Fin sighed. "We talked about past stuff and why he didn't ever come see me play. Dunno, just upset us both. Don't even know why I started it. I upset Da and myself and I still don't really understand."

Running his fingers through Fin's black curls, Mick kissed the top of his head. "You started it because you know you need the answers before he goes. Nothing wrong with that. At least you're trying to understand." He ran his hands down Fin's arms and held his hands. "Did ya get a chance to watch a game with him?"

"Yeah. We watched the Rose Bowl game. Da asked me about strategy and plays and stuff. It was pretty cool. He fell asleep before it was over but it was enough." Fin looked up into Mick's eyes. "I'm calling hospice tomorrow. Da's in pain even though he won't tell us. Maybe they can give him something."

Mick held Fin's head in his hands. "It signifies the beginning of the end. You know that, don't you? Once they start giving him morphine he won't be as coherent as he is now. He may say things that upset you or that you don't understand and he won't be able to explain himself. You need to make peace as soon as possible, okay?"

With tears rolling down his cheeks, Fin nodded. "Yeah. I get that. The thing is…I don't think he'll ever be able to tell me any more than he already has. I know it's up to me to work out my feelings."

Mick wiped Fin's face. "I love you, baby."

"Love you. You'd better get back to work." Fin gave him a little grin. "I came here with a quickie in mind but the way I'm feeling I think I'd rather wait until I can get you in my bed."

Mick kissed him once more and stood up. "Come on. I'll buy ya a beer and sing for you before you head home." He held Fin's hand all the way down the stairs. Just before he opened the door he pulled Fin into his arms once more. "We'll get through this."

"Would you sing 'The Banks of Lee' for me? You sang it the first night I met you. I think it's when I started falling in love with you."

"You bet."

* * * * *

When Mick tiptoed into the bedroom later that night Fin was sound asleep and snoring up a storm. Mick would have laughed if he hadn't just found Sean sitting up in bed in pain and trying to catch his breath. He gave him a pain pill and sat with him until he finally managed to fall asleep. Mick had placed a kiss on Sean's forehead and uttered a quick prayer before heading up to be with his love. Fin was right. It was time to call in the professionals.

Mick thought all evening about the pub and what Sean wanted to do with it after he passed. He knew Fin wanted nothing to do with it and although he could easily buy it from him, Mick knew he couldn't work there day in and day out with Sean's presence everywhere.

He even thought maybe he'd follow Fin back to New York for the last two years on his contract but in the end he knew it would lead to resentment on his part. He just couldn't be hidden away like a secret. Mick finally decided he'd probably go back to the house on the bluff. What he'd do after that was anyone's guess.

He undressed and crawled into bed beside the snoring monster. Mick glanced at the clock, almost four-thirty. Shit, no wonder he was so tired. He decided to curl up against Fin and get a couple hours of sleep before waking him. From now on they might have to take sleep when they could get it.

Scooting his back against Fin's front, he settled in for the night. Fin pulled him even closer and kissed his neck without waking up. It gave Mick a warm feeling to know Fin loved him even in his sleep. He yawned and shut his eyes.

He felt a deliciously hot mouth surrounding his morning wood. "Mmm…"

He cracked open his eyes and looked down at Fin. He spread his legs a little farther apart and let Fin continue his ministrations. The swirling of Fin's tongue caused a moan to escape and Fin's eyes smiled up at him. He pulled his mouth off Mick's cock with a pop.

"Mornin', sweetheart." He crawled up beside Mick and pulled him into his arms. "Why didn't you wake me when you got in?" Fin started rubbing his own erection against his.

"It was four-thirty by the time I got to bed. I was too tired to play and you were snoring like a grizzly bear." He ran his hands up Fin's back.

"Why four-thirty? I thought you got off a little after two?" Fin started to grind against him a little more.

"Sean was up and in pain when I got home. I gave him a pill and sat with him until he went back to sleep." Mick managed a glance at the clock. Damn, it was almost nine o'clock. Sean was probably due for another pill by now. He hated to do it but Mick knew he had to hurry Fin up so he could get downstairs. He brought his hand to his mouth and licked three fingers. Reaching down, he rimmed Fin's hole before inserting first one then two fingers.

"Oh Christ." Fin rubbed against him faster and Mick slipped the third finger in. Fin shot his heat between their two bodies.

Mick followed quickly with Fin's name on his lips. They cuddled for another couple of minutes kissing and touching while whispering words of love. Mick rose up and kissed Fin. "I need to grab a quick shower and check on Sean. He probably needs another pain pill by now." He swung his legs over the side of the bed. "You're right about calling the hospice, by the way. Do you want to do it or should I?"

It took Fin a couple moments to answer. "I'll do it."

Mick nodded and made his way to the shower. It said a lot about Fin's mood that he didn't join him. By the time Mick got out of the shower and made it downstairs Fin had breakfast on the table.

He looked over his shoulder at Mick. "I gave Da a pill. I'm not sure how long he had been lying there needing it though. I'll call for more help after breakfast."

Mick could see the guilt in Fin's stiff posture. He walked over and rested a hand on his shoulder. "You can't blame yourself, Fin. We'll just have to be a little more diligent from now on." Mick let go and sat down at the table. "Do you know if Sean wants anything to eat this morning?"

Fin shook his head without even looking at Mick. "He's already gone back to sleep but he said he wasn't hungry earlier." He finished buttering Mick's toast and set the plate on the table. Taking his chair, Fin bowed his head and said a prayer before eating.

Chapter Nine

✆

Two days later Fin was sitting at his da's bedside reading his new playbook that'd come in the mail. The coach was starting to get a little concerned that Fin wouldn't be able to learn everything and get into condition before training camp. That was still two weeks away and by the way his da was breathing Fin knew he'd be gone before training camp began.

"What…are…you…reading?" Sean was barely able to speak.

Fin's head snapped up and raised the front of the book. "I got my new playbook this afternoon. They're adding a lot of new plays this season. I just hope they work."

"So…proud…Calder." A tear leaked down his cheek. "I wish…I had…one…more…season left."

Fin closed his eyes and hugged his da. "I'll play this season for you, Da. You can watch me from heaven with Mom." Fin knew it was a hokey thing to say but it brightened his da's eyes for just a moment before he fell back asleep.

* * * * *

Three nights later, after a physically exhausting lovemaking session with Mick, he had a strange feeling. He looked down at Mick who was almost asleep in his arms. Fin bent and kissed Mick softly. "You sleep. I'm going downstairs and sit with Da for a while."

Mick mumbled something Fin didn't understand and ran his hand down Fin's face. Fin smiled and kissed his cheek. He took his pillow and went down to sit with his da. The night-light beside Sean's bed made it easy for Fin to make his way to the recliner. He dumped his pillow and went to the living room to get the dark blue afghan his mom had crocheted.

He settled into the recliner with his pillow and blanket and listened to his da fight to breathe. As he listened, he found himself matching his da's breathing. Before long Fin felt lightheaded. "How do you do it, Da?" he whispered into the darkness. Fin got back up and pushed the chair closer to the bed. After resettling himself he reached out and held his da's hand. It felt so small and frail in his big hand. The skin was paper thin and mottled with bruises He thought of the past and compared it to the last couple of weeks. He suddenly realized that his da was just an ordinary man who'd made bad choices but had tried his damndest to make up for them in the end.

Fin thought of all the mistakes he'd made in his life. What if he had a son who held a microscope up to every one of his past mistakes? With tears in his eyes he suddenly realized that the past was gone. His da had always loved him and been proud of him. He just hadn't known how to show it.

Fin felt peace overcome him. He'd not only gotten to know his da but he'd learned to like him. It was just too bad they'd both been stubborn for so many years. Fin looked at his da in the dim glow of the night-light.

The more he sat there and listened to his da try to breathe, the more he was sure of what he needed to do. He needed to let his da go in peace. Fin stood and pushed the recliner out of the way. He tried to scoot his da over as gently as possible. After making room, Fin crawled into the narrow hospital bed beside him. He took a deep calming breath and wrapped his arms around the now-frail man. Fin held his da and cried as the darkness surrounded them.

When Fin's tears became audible sobs Sean opened his eyes. He looked at his son and put his hand on Fin's cheek. "Lo...ve you."

"I love you too, Da. I always have. It's time, Da. Time for you to go meet up with Mom. Your girl has been waiting for you for a long time. Show her the eternity she deserves. I'll be all right. I have Mick and I've a feeling he's not going to let me get too far away from him. When you see Mom," Fin's voice cracked as he thought of her, "tell her I love her and that you and I are okay now. We've made our peace. Your work here is done and I can't stand to see you in pain anymore." Fin bent and kissed his da's cheek and held him as tightly as he dared.

Sean put his hand on Fin's. "Than...k you, Cal...der."

Fin felt his da slip back into sleep. He knew in his heart that he'd be gone by morning. Fin stayed awake, just holding and whispering words of love to his da.

* * * * *

Mick woke with a start. Looking around the bedroom, he couldn't figure out what woke him. He looked at the clock. It was only four o'clock in the morning. Suddenly he realized that Fin wasn't in bed with him. He vaguely remembered Fin telling him he was going to sit with Sean.

He swung his legs over the side of the bed and slipped into a pair of sweats. As he made his way downstairs, the hair on the back of his neck began to prickle. He entered the study quietly.

Fin was curled around Sean in the hospital bed. He was holding his father, crying. He began to rock the old man and it dawned on Mick that he didn't hear the hiss of the oxygen tank. He walked closer to the bed. "Fin, why isn't the oxygen on?"

Fin looked up at him and he knew. Sean was already gone. Mick dropped to his knees beside the bed and he too began to cry. He thought of all the discussions he and Sean had had over the years. All the wisdom Sean tried to impart. All the stupid games of poker they'd played on a slow night at the pub. After several long minutes he reached up and pulled himself to his feet again. Mick felt completely numb. He knew he needed to pull himself together for Fin but Fin seemed to be right where he needed to be, for now.

Fin looked down the bed at Mick. "About twenty minutes ago. He squeezed my hand one last time and I knew. He told me he loved me earlier and I told him I forgave him and it was time for him to go to Mom."

Fin reached for his hand and Mick offered it. "What do we do now? Should we wait to call the funeral home or do we call the hospice or what?"

Mick kissed Fin's palm. "Now we clean him up and say our goodbyes. Afterward, we call the hospice. They'll send someone over."

Mick stood and walked around to Fin's side of the bed. "Come on, baby, let's get some clean pajamas and a basin of hot soapy water. Sean wouldn't want anyone seeing him like this."

Fin nodded and Mick got a half-smile. "He always was too proud for his own damn good."

* * * * *

The memorial service was held five days later at Finnegan's. Sean requested that he be cremated and put in the same plot as Fin's mom. Fin purchased a black marble bench with his da's name and the appropriate dates etched on the top. When it was ready it would sit at the end of his mom's grave.

Mick went with Fin the night before under cover of darkness to dig the tiny hole beside his mother's headstone. Fin knew it was wrong to have more than one person buried in a plot but it was his da's wishes. They placed the biodegradable carton with his da's ashes into the hole and covered it with dirt and a bouquet of roses.

Fin sat at the bar and listened to his da's old friends tell stories about the man he'd just recently grown to know. He watched Mick serve up drinks and add a few stories of his own. He had to leave in two days to get ready for training camp. Two days until he said goodbye to Mick. He'd tried several times to get Mick to move to New York but he was adamant about living in his house up the coast.

They'd hired Jesse as a full-time manager for the pub. It was a hard sell because Jesse still had one more year of college left but when they told him he could live in the loft and hire an assistant manager for the day shift he finally agreed.

They both knew they'd never want to run the pub themselves again but neither one of them would think of selling Finnegan's. As long as the pub doors remained open Sean Finnegan's legacy would live on.

One of his da's regulars took up a collection and had a barstool made with Sean's name carved into the wood. It now sat at the end of the bar. Fin bet that stool would remain empty no matter how crowded the pub became. Fin ran his fingers over the mahogany stool. "You've always got a place here, Da."

Fin took another sip of his coffee. He searched out Mick again with his eyes. Mick stopped what he was doing and looked Fin's way. The two of them had moved back upstairs to the loft after the funeral home had taken Sean's body away. Fin pointed up and Mick nodded and held up a finger.

Saying a few last words to Jesse, Mick made his way over to Fin. "Are you ready to go on up?"

"Yes. I need to take a bath and unwind." Fin looked at Mick.

Mick seemed to understand that Fin needed some time alone. "I'll be up as soon as everyone leaves. Probably be another hour or so."

Fin nodded and squeezed Mick's hand. "I'll see ya then."

* * * * *

It was an hour and a half before Mick got everyone out. Mel and Jesse volunteered to clean up and lock the pub for him so he headed upstairs.

He found Fin on the couch naked, looking through Mick's photo album. He undressed and took a quick shower after dropping a kiss on Fin's forehead.

After he was clean and dry he headed naked to the couch. He sat beside Fin and put his arm around him. "Lookin' at all my dorky kid pictures, babe?"

Fin gave him a half-smile. "I wanted to see a picture of your mom. What was her name? I don't think you ever told me."

Mick flipped to his mom's senior picture, it was his favorite. "Erin. It's Gaelic for Ireland."

"She was beautiful, Mick." Fin leaned over and kissed him.

"She was beautiful both inside and out. I know you don't feel like it right now but you were lucky that you got a chance to say your final goodbyes to your da before he died. I'd give anything for five more minutes with my mom just to tell her how much I loved her."

Fin put the album on the coffee table and stood. He pulled Mick up into his arms. "Let's go to bed, sweetheart."

Fin led Mick into the bedroom and pulled back the covers. They slid in and right into each other's arms. Kissing and rubbing, they loved each other slowly. Fin kissed every inch of Mick's body. He wanted to memorize every detail about Mick. "Please come back to New York with me, Mick."

Mick closed his eyes. "I can't. We have a better chance of making it if I don't go and you know that. Why can't you skip the rest of your contract and move up the coast with me? I don't think your heart is really in it anymore anyway."

Swallowing around the lump in his throat, Fin shook his head. "I promised my da the night he died I'd dedicate this season to him. He seemed…proud. I can't go back on my word to him."

Mick ran his hand down the length of Fin's torso. He lightly ran his fingers up and down the length of Fin's cock. "Well then, I guess I only have a day and half to convince you that you can't live without me."

"You don't need a day and a half for that. I already know I can't live without you or haven't you been listening?" Fin rolled over on top of Mick and began kissing him again. "Tonight I want you to make love to me. I need to feel you inside me." With that said Fin rolled them both over so Mick was on top.

Mick knew what Fin was needing. He'd only let Mick fuck him a couple of times since they'd been together. Mick started slow, kissing and stroking Fin. He licked and nipped at his nipples and neck, slowly grinding his cock against Fin's as the passion built higher and higher.

He reached for the bottle of lube and with gentle fingers expertly stretched Fin. Fin moaned and pushed into his fingers. "Now, sweetheart."

Mick carefully entered Fin, watching for any signs of pain or distress. The only look on Fin's face was a look of complete pleasure. Mick moved his hips back and forth while kissing him. He gradually built the pace until Fin lifted his legs and put them over Mick's shoulders.

He knew that was the sign that Fin needed to come. Mick started pumping a little harder and a little faster. He watched Fin reach down and begin stroking his own cock.

Fin pumped his cock faster. "Need it…gonna…love you." Fin's stomach muscles clenched as he erupted onto his hand and chest.

Mick picked up the pace even more. "Love… Mine." He pushed in one last time and exploded his heat inside the man he loved. He collapsed on top of Fin and immediately fell into a deep sleep.

* * * * *

Packing his bags, Fin looked around the loft for anything he might have forgotten. He was bone tired, having made love throughout the night. Mick still asleep, looked like he'd been ridden hard and put away wet. Fin smiled, remembering the chocolate pudding Mick brought to the bedroom. He'd never be able to eat chocolate pudding again without thinking of Mick.

They hadn't made any promises to each other, just that they would keep in touch. Fin worried that he was giving up too much for only two more years of football but a promise was a promise. He'd already cleaned out the tapes in Da's office and had them shipped to his apartment in New York. The house would be sold as soon as he could go through everything but he was running short on time and drive. He knew his da didn't want him to sell it but Fin could never live there so what was the point. Keeping the pub was going to be hard enough to handle.

He found a pair of socks under the couch in the living room and a couple of t-shirts in the dirty clothes hamper. Returning them to his suitcase, he glanced once again toward the bed. Mick's eyes were open, watching him. Fin dropped the clothes into the suitcase and went to sit on the side of the bed. He leaned over and kissed him. "Morning, sweetheart."

"What time is your flight?" Mick kissed him back and squeezed his hand.

"I've got to leave in an hour. The flight's at eleven." Fin looked into Mick's blue eyes. He still had so many questions about their future, how could he leave? "I can call you, right? Maybe come see you when I get a chance?"

Mick kissed his palm. "You'll always be welcome in my home, baby, and yes, you'd better call me." Mick shifted and sat up. He opened his arms and Fin fell into them. "I might even sneak in to a game once or twice."

Fin felt a ray of hope. "You'll let me know, won't you, and I can get you tickets? I haven't had anyone come watch me since Mom died." The feelings of loneliness started to resurface but Fin pushed them away.

Mick put his hand on Fin's cheek. "If I come I'd better just buy a regular ticket like everyone else. What would people think if I were to sit in the wife and girlfriend section, Fin?" Mick shook his head. "It would be better to just be part of the crowd. No one would get suspicious that way."

Knowing Mick was right, Fin closed his eyes. He made a momentous decision on the spot. "This will be my last year if I can get out of my contract. I'll play this year for Da and then maybe you'll still want me." With hope in his heart he looked into Mick's eyes.

Mick leaned in and kissed him. "I'll always want you, but a lot can happen in a year. What if you meet someone else?"

"No. I'll never meet anyone else that I want more than you, Mick. Ever." He stood and pulled off his t-shirt and pushed down his faded jeans. His cock sprang free of his underwear and he crawled under the covers. He pulled Mick into his arms. "I wish you could understand how important this season is to me."

Tears pooled in Mick's blue eyes. "I do understand. I'm just feeling selfish at the moment." Mick laid his head on Fin's chest and outlined the defined muscles with his finger.

Fin kissed the top of Mick's head and ran his hands down his back. "Maybe you should think of recording some of your Irish ballads while I'm away. You've got the studio already." He tilted Mick's head up to look into his eyes. "There's a difference between singing because you love it and doing it just to make money."

Crawling on top of Fin, Mick licked the side of his face. "I've already been thinkin' about it. I guess I could record and just not tour. The touring part is what got me into trouble before. I miss singing though."

Taking both their cocks in his hand, Fin gave them a gentle pull. "Why don't you record the songs while I'm gone and then when I'm finished with the season we can travel around the country and you could sing in pubs? That's where you're the happiest anyway." Fin continued the soft rub to their cocks.

Mick started moving against Fin's hand, making him speed up the pace. "I'm the happiest with you. I'll think about it though."

Enough talking, Fin thought, and took Mick's mouth in a searing kiss. He thrust his cock against Mick's and buried a finger in Mick's ass. Heat sprayed onto his stomach as Mick moaned and grunted his orgasm. Fin continued kissing him while his own orgasm shook him. He shuddered as he pumped his seed between them. Hopefully it would be the only thing that ever came between them.

Chapter Ten

80

Training camp had been a bitch. Fin had to work twice as hard to get his body back in shape after a month and a half of fattening food and beer. The only thing that got him through was his nightly calls to Mick.

He decided he'd work out and train every minute he was off the field. Not that his body was that out of shape but Fin wanted to have his best season ever. He'd played every preseason game like his da and mom were there with him watching.

Fin walked into his Manhattan apartment and threw his keys on the entry table. He looked around at the modest one-bedroom apartment. He'd lived here for almost seven years and had yet to put up any kind of pictures or fancy doodads like his mom had. It had always just been the place where he slept, never his home.

He walked into the living room and picked up the phone. He speed-dialed Mick's number and loosened his tie. He hated getting dressed up for game day. It was only out of respect for his team and the game that he continued to do it. He tore off the tie and unbuttoned his shirt, waiting for Mick to pick up. The answering machine finally clicked on and Fin's hopes of talking to Mick fell. "Hi, sweetheart, just called to talk. Call me back as soon as you can." He hung up the phone and headed for the shower, taking the cordless phone with him just in case.

Fin showered and fixed bacon and eggs for dinner. He ate alone in front of the television. He kept glancing at the phone, willing it to ring. Finally at nine o'clock he grabbed the phone and called Mick again.

"Hello," a strange deep voice answered. Fin pulled the phone away from his ear and checked the phone number he'd called. Yep, it was the right number but the wrong voice. "Is Mick there?"

"He's in the shower. Can I tell him who called?"

Fin felt like a lead weight dropped smack-dab down on his chest. "No. I'll try back another time." Fin hung up the phone without waiting for a reply. "Fuck." He couldn't believe Mick had another man at his house at nine o'clock at night. He threw the phone against the wall and ran to the bathroom to throw up.

He brushed his teeth and grabbed a bottle of Irish whiskey, taking it back to bed with him. Fin got totally and thoroughly drunk. He heard the phone ring several times but was in no mood to talk to Mick.

The next morning he felt like something had crawled into his mouth and died. He sat up in bed and then raced once again to the toilet. Damn, he knew whiskey made him sick. He brushed his teeth and crawled back into bed.

Two hours later the phone started ringing again. He woke up and picked up the phone. "I've nothing to say." Fin hung the phone up and unplugged it. He felt like his whole world was collapsing and he didn't even have enough energy to get out of bed. He burrowed back under the covers and fell asleep again.

He woke four hours later to a pounding on the door. Fin held his head, wishing the noise would stop, but it didn't. He managed to get out of bed and pull on his white terry robe. Still holding his head, he made his way to the door. "Who is it?" he yelled through the door.

"Open up, Fin!" Mick's voice sounded as pissed off as his did.

Fin closed his eyes and swung the door open. "I told you I've nothing to say." He started to shut the door as Mick pushed it back open and pushed Fin into the apartment.

"Well, that's too damn bad 'cause I've got something to say to you, asshole!" Mick walked into the living room and paced back and forth. "I've come all this way and I'm not leaving until you hear me the fuck out."

Fin went over and sat on the edge of the couch. "So talk."

"Jay told me you called so why wouldn't you answer the phone when I called back and why the hell did you hang up on me this morning?" The veins in Mick's forehead were bulging. Fin thought he might have a stroke or something.

"Why don't you tell me who the hell Jay is and why the hell he was at your house at nine o'clock at night with you in the shower?" Fin stood toe to toe with Mick, fists clenched at his side.

"Jay's the guy I hired to help me make the recordings of my songs, asshole. We'd spent all day in the studio working and I was hot and sweaty so I took a fuckin' shower. Jay told me you called just before he left." Mick shook his head as if he couldn't believe they were fighting over this. "You know we're fucked if you don't even trust me enough to ask me about something instead of just assuming it's so."

Fin closed his eyes and swallowed around the lump in his throat. "So tell me you and this Jay have nothin' going on?" Fin wanted to believe it so badly. The thought of Mick with someone else made him want to throw up again.

Mick rubbed his forehead and ran his hands through his hair. "Jay's a married man in his fifties but even if he was a single gorgeous gay man I wouldn't have anything besides music going on with him. It's you I love, you bastard." Mick threw himself on the couch.

Fin sighed. Fuck, he'd really screwed up this time. "I love you too. I'm sorry I jumped to conclusions like that. You're the only person in the world I have left. I guess maybe I'm just paranoid about losing you." He walked over and sat beside Mick on the couch. He held his hand out to Mick. "Can you forgive me please?"

After a few tense seconds Mick put his hand in Fin's. "Never think that I'll cheat on you. I wouldn't do it in a million years and until you really believe it you'll always have doubts about me. I won't live that way. I've got a few more musicians and sound engineers scheduled to come in this week and I won't be paranoid that one of them might answer the damn phone."

He pulled Mick into his arms and kissed him. "I was so heartbroken I drank an entire bottle of Irish whiskey last night." He kissed down the side of Mick's neck and sucked up a mark. "I love you. Days like this I want to just quit my job and go home with you."

Mick shook his head. "I've watched the preseason games and you're playing better than ever. I think you were right. You do need this last season."

"I don't need it as much as I need you." Fin shook his head and closed his eyes.

Mick licked the sole tear sliding down Fin's face. "Luckily you don't have to choose between us. I'll still be here when the season is over and then we can start our life together."

Fin stood and carried Mick to his bedroom. Mick looked around the room as he undressed. "Not much for decorating, huh, Fin?"

That got a smile out of him. "No need to decorate when you don't have company. I think you might be the first person to ever see this apartment."

Mick slid into Fin's queen-sized bed. "I think you'd be happier if you tried to make at least one friend here in New York." He winked at Fin. "As long as it's a straight friend. No sense in tempting you too much."

Fin shrugged out of his robe and crawled on top of Mick. "I'll be fine now that I know I've got you on my side." He licked the hickey he'd given Mick earlier and ran his hands down Mick's chest to pinch his hardened nipples. He ran his tongue around Mick's chest, just tasting the saltiness of his skin.

He looked up at Mick. "I've been thinkin' about getting a tattoo. Something to remind me of both of us."

Mick licked his lips and tweaked Fin's nipple. "That sounds sexy as hell. What were you thinking of?"

Fin ran his finger over Mick's heart. "Not sure yet. I'll surprise you someday with it." He began grinding his cock into Mick's leg.

Mick pulled on Fin's arm. "C'mere you."

Crawling back up Mick's body, Fin took his mouth as he ground his cock against Mick's. "Love you."

Moaning and thrusting up, Mick nodded. "Need you, baby." Mick did his best imitation of an octopus and wrapped his legs around Fin as his hands touched every available surface.

Fin nodded and reached for his bedside table. Digging around in the drawer he produced a bottle of lube. "Turn over and let me make love to you."

Smiling, Mick rolled over and sat up on his hands and knees. Wiggling his ass at Fin, Mick proudly presented his hole. "It's all yours."

"Mmm," Fin moaned as he licked a path up and down the crevice of Mick's ass. "So pretty," he mumbled as he rimmed the hole with his tongue. Fin felt nothing but skin on the cleanly waxed ass. "Taste so good, sweetheart." He placed an open-mouthed kiss to Mick's hole, flicking his tongue just inside the rosette and reached for the lube.

After squirting lube directly into Mick's hole, Fin bit Mick's butt cheek. "I'm going to make you feel so good." He pushed in one finger and smiled at Mick's moan of pleasure. Adding another finger, Fin reached around and stroked Mick's cock. "No one but you." Fin found Mick's prostate gland and pegged it with a brush of his finger.

Mick's back bowed. "Now, baby. Need you."

Picking up the lube, Fin quickly slicked his cock and positioned himself at Mick's opening. He started to enter him slowly when Mick took matters into his own hands and pushed back, burying Fin's cock to the root. "Shit," Fin yelled as Mick continued to move on his cock.

Reaching out, Fin ran his hands down Mick's sweaty back. He scraped the delicate looking skin with his fingernails and got hotter as he watched the red marks appear. "Marking you as mine."

Turning his head around to look back at Fin, Mick grunted, "Yours," as he continued to move at a faster pace. Fin placed his hands on Mick's hips and pounded Mick's ass as hard and fast as he could. He heard Mick shout his release and felt the tightening of Mick's muscles around his cock but Fin was in the zone. He continued to fuck Mick even after Mick's front half collapsed on the bed.

Mick turned his head to watch him and Fin knew that without the promise to his da, he'd quit professional football tomorrow for this man. Mick reached back toward Fin and mouthed the words, "I love you." Fin pushed in once more and came growling Mick's name.

Falling to the bed beside Mick, Fin put his hand to his chest. "I think you've nearly killed me, but damn, what a way to go."

* * * * *

Fin managed to get Thanksgiving off so he flew to the small Rockport airport and had Mick pick him up. Getting off the plane, he spotted Mick immediately. He smiled and tipped his baseball cap. Mick smiled back and waited for him to get through the crowd.

Damn, Mick looked good. It had been two months since they'd seen each other although they still talked almost nightly on the phone. "Hey, sweetheart," Fin said in a soft voice that only Mick could hear. "I've missed you."

Mick squeezed his shoulder. "Missed you too, baby. Come on, let's get home so I can welcome you properly." He gestured down to the little overnight bag in Fin's hand. "Is that all you brought?"

Fin held up the bag. "Afraid so. Gotta be back for a meeting on Saturday evening but you've got me 'til then."

Mick led him out to the parking lot. They climbed into his white SUV and headed down the coast to Mick's house. Mick reached over the console and held Fin's hand. "Missed you so much."

Fin kissed the back of his hand. "Missed you too. The season's almost over though and it doesn't look like we'll be getting too far in the playoffs this year. Most of our best players are on the injured list."

Mick squeezed his hand again. "Don't get modest on me. You're the best player on the team and everyone knows it. You're well on the way to breaking a couple of records this season. Sean would be proud of you, Fin."

"Thanks. I feel him every time I step onto the field. It's like he's right there with me giving me speed every time I run for a touchdown." Fin shrugged like it was no big deal but he suspected Mick knew he was just being modest.

"Have you talked to the management about retiring yet?"

"I had my agent tell the owners but I told the offensive and head coaches. Everyone thinks I'm just after more money no matter how much I deny it. They don't have a clue that I never played for the money anyway."

Mick pulled up to the house and turned off the car. "I sent the musicians and my sound engineer home yesterday so we'll have the whole place to ourselves." He leaned over the console and finally got the kiss he'd been waitin' on.

Fin held the back of Mick's head and deepened the kiss. "Inside. I need you naked."

They both got out of the car and ran up the porch steps. Mick unlocked the door and the two of them fell onto the floor in the entry in a tangle of arms and legs.

Pulling his polo over his head, Fin waited for Mick to see his tattoo. He didn't have to wait long.

"Oh fuck." Mick reached out his hand and traced the tattoo over his heart. "What does it mean?"

Fin looked down at his chest. It was a picture of an old football leaning against a well-used fiddle. "It looks pretty simple, I know, but the real meaning gets pretty complicated."

"Tell me."

"In my case the football symbolizes my need for acceptance from my da and the lengths I was willing to go to get it. The fiddle symbolizes you of course and your rise to fame although I know you did it for different reasons. The fact still remains that neither of these things made us happy because we were both doing it for the wrong reasons. This is the first year that I'm actually playing not only for my da but also for me. It's cleansed me in a way that nothing else could. I feel free of all the past disappointments and pain."

Fin leaned in for a kiss. "Now it's your turn, Mick. You need to start playing your fiddle again."

Mick narrowed his eyes and shook his head. "No. I've already told you I'll never play again. My fiddle is full of grief, remember? If I play it won't sound the same to me."

Fin bracketed Mick's face with his hands. "Don't you get it? A fiddle can't hold grief. Your grief is still locked up inside your heart. Playing your fiddle can cleanse your soul just like playing football this season has cleansed mine."

"Maybe I'm not ready to let go of my grief yet because the thought of picking up that instrument tears me apart."

Fin decided to let the subject drop for now. "Anyway that's what the tat stands for. I guess you think it's pretty silly, huh?"

"Not silly at all. It's a beautiful tattoo and a beautiful thought. I'm just not ready to let go yet...that's all."

Fin stood and pulled Mick into his arms. "Feed me please. I haven't eaten since breakfast." He looked around the house. "Hey, do I smell turkey?"

Mick smiled and pulled him toward the kitchen. "Yep. I'm making a full Thanksgiving Day feast just for us. If you want to help me peel potatoes we can finish everything up and eat and then watch a movie." He bumped hips with Fin. "Or something."

* * * * *

They both sprawled on the couch with their jeans unbuttoned. Fin rubbed his extended stomach. "I haven't eaten a Thanksgiving dinner like that since Mom died. I don't think I'll be able to move for the rest of the day."

Mick smiled and nudged Fin's ass with his foot. "I'm countin' on you moving as soon as this movie is done. I'm not feeding you dessert until I get mine." He winked.

"Yeah, I hear ya but give me another thirty minutes at least."

"'Kay."

Fin spread his arms and crooked his finger. "C'mere, you could at least snuggle with me. Maybe we could even get a little snooze in."

That seemed to make Mick much happier. The man was sex-starved evidently. They'd already made love in the kitchen and rubbed each other off before they sat down to eat dinner but Mick was still looking for more.

They snuggled up together on the couch and after a few sweet kisses fell asleep.

Waking with a hot mouth wrapped around your cock was a very good thing, Fin decided. He cracked an eye open and looked down. Mick was petting and purring, just swallowing his cock over and over. He reached down and ran his fingers through Mick's hair. "Your hair's getting long, Mick." As he said it he thrust up, driving his cock even deeper into the hot mouth.

"Mmm…" was the only response Mick gave. Fin enjoyed the view of Mick's head bobbing up and down. Watching his dark swollen cock disappear into the hidden depths of Mick's mouth was winding him up. He reached down and ran his fingers around the stretched skin of Mick's mouth.

Pulling off Fin's cock, he nuzzled his way down to Fin's sac. Rolling first one ball and then the other around in his mouth, Mick started fisting his own cock. "Need inside."

Grunting, Fin flipped himself over onto his hands and knees and presented his ass to Mick. With no lube in sight and not willing to leave the couch Mick licked the darkly shaded pucker. He swirled as much saliva as he could into the hole and spat into his own hand to lube his cock. Leaning over Fin's back, he pushed in slowly, not wanting to hurt his love.

Mick pushed through the tight ring of muscles and worked himself in until his balls rested against Fin's ass. "Tight. Been too long." He started to move slowly at first then building speed and pressure.

Fin pushed back, grunting. "More."

Mick licked up his spine and bit at his shoulder. "Mine."

"Yours."

He stroked Fin's cock with one hand while holding on to his hip with the other. Mick changed positions and found Fin's prostate.

"Oh fuck. Right there." Fin's head was thrown back and he pounded back against Mick's cock. "Can't wait…gonna blow."

Mick moved his hand from Fin's hip and thrust one finger inside the already stretched hole to push against the gland. Pumping Fin's cock as fast as he could, they both came screaming each other's name.

Fin fell to the couch with Mick landing on top of him. "Love you."

Mick kissed his shoulder. "You too, baby."

"I wanna listen to some of your music." Fin turned his head to the side to get a kiss.

Mick rose up so they could lie side by side on the deep couch. He traced Fin's tattoo as he nodded. "We've been getting a lot done. The songs aren't top forty, just simple Irish pub songs."

Leaning in for another kiss, Fin smiled. "That's good, sweetheart, because I love your pub songs. The guys on the team make fun of me because I listen to the CD you gave me before every game." He shrugged his shoulders. "Helps get me ready to play."

That got a big smile out of Mick. "I'll have to send you home with some others then. You've got some big games coming up." He squirmed against Fin.

Fin raised his eyebrow and chuckled. "I've got somethin' else coming up too." He pushed back against Mick.

Laughing, Mick swatted his shoulder. "Don't use it all up now. We've still got another day together." He stood up and pulled on Fin's hand. "Up. Let's go to the studio, maybe I can talk you into making a recording for me." He led Fin by the hand toward the studio.

"I don't sing worth shit and you know it."

Looking back over his shoulder, Mick winked. "I don't need you to sing. Just talk dirty to me in that deep sexy voice of yours. I can play it while I jack off when you're away."

"I can do that. You're easy to talk dirty to."

* * * * *

Saturday morning he woke to the smell of frying bacon. His stomach growled, letting him know he was starving. Fin sat up in bed and scratched his chest and looked at the clock. It

Carol Lynne

was almost ten o'clock. Damn, he had to leave for the airport in two hours. He couldn't believe the time had gone so fast.

Standing up, he felt a sharp pain in his knee. He fell back onto the bed and rubbed at it. He'd hurt it a month earlier in a game but hadn't told Mick. He knew he'd insist that Fin sit out a few games and let it heal but Fin planned to play the season until the end. The team trainer was giving him regular shots of cortisone to help the swelling and pain but by the looks of his knee he might have to figure something else out by Sunday.

Fin hurried into the shower, putting most of his weight on his right leg. He needed to shower quickly and get dressed before Mick came in and saw the swelling. Wrapping his knee in a tight bandage, he slipped on his jeans and headed for the kitchen. He found breakfast in the warming oven but no sign of Mick.

He looked out the window toward the bluff. Mick was standing looking out over the ocean with a cup of coffee in hand. He looked so beautiful with the wind blowing his overly long hair around his face. Fin wanted so bad to go to him but he knew his knee wasn't up to walking on the uneven ground. Instead he opened the back door and called to Mick. "Hey, are you comin' in for breakfast?"

Turning around, Mick smiled and headed his way. Fin got the plates out of the oven and set them on the table. He poured himself a cup of coffee and sat down, stretching his sore knee out in front of him. He only had to hide it for another hour and a half.

Mick came in the back door and bent to give him a kiss. "Morning, sleepyhead." He sat down across from Fin after refilling his coffee cup.

"Sorry about that. Someone must've kept me awake late last night." He grinned at Mick and took a drink of coffee. "I need to leave at noon to catch my flight."

"I know. I wish you could stay but I know you can't." Mick looked at him a few more seconds then shook his head and started eating his breakfast.

Fin reached across the table and took his hand. "Won't be long now, sweetheart, and you'll have me in your hair every day."

Mick squeezed his hand. "Never soon enough for me, baby."

* * * * *

Mick dropped Fin off at the airport at noon. They both decided it was better if they said their goodbyes in the car instead of in front of a terminal full of people. Waving one last time, he pulled away from the curb and headed home. He needed to take care of a few things before heading into New York himself.

He'd kept it to himself but he'd gone to almost every one of Fin's games this season. Sitting in the stands, he felt so proud of Fin for working through his grief. He'd known even before Fin had told him, this season was cleansing him. He could see the grief fading every time Fin made another run for a touchdown. He'd been right. He did need this season to heal.

Mick's jaw tightened at the thought of Fin's knee. He'd seen it happen. He knew Fin was in pain and yet he still played. Mick only wished Fin had talked to him about it instead of trying to hide it from him.

He thought about the tattoo over Fin's heart. The symbolism was deeper than the tattoo itself. He wondered if Fin was right about playing his fiddle. He hadn't even taken it out of the case since he played for his mom that last time.

When he got home he walked to the bedroom closet and lifted the case from the top shelf. Taking it over to the bed, he sat down with the dusty case in his lap. The black leather case looked its years, old and starting to crack along the seams. The fiddle had belonged to his grandfather. He'd always wished he'd gotten a chance to meet him but he died just before Mick was born. It was the fiddle his mother had taught him to play on.

No matter how much money he made he never even thought about replacing it. The music it emitted was really sweet. Mick always thought it was because it had been played with love for so long. The thought brought him up short. How had he taken an instrument of love and turned it into a vessel of grief?

He thought about his mother, wishing she were here to guide him. Would she be happy that he refused to play after her death? No, he didn't think she would. Mick looked down at the case on his lap and slowly unlatched it. He opened the lid and ran his fingers over the neglected strings. Funny thing, when he touched the fiddle he didn't feel grief. He felt his mom's and his grandfather's presence but not grief.

Closing the lid, he knew he had a lot of work to do. He needed to pack an overnight bag and head to the city. He always preferred to drive instead of taking a plane. He put his bags into his SUV and headed for New Jersey.

Chapter Eleven

ຂວ

Mick watched in horror as the next two games Fin played punished his already injured knee. The fans in the stands and watching on television weren't aware of the pain he was in but Mick could tell by the sound of his voice on the phone every night. He needed only three more rushing touchdowns to beat his own record set during his third year in the pros. With only three games left and a bum knee the odds were quickly stacking up against him.

Mick got home from Jacksonville around eleven o'clock that night and decided to wait until morning to call Fin. He undressed and got his favorite CD out and put it into his CD player. Taking the portable CD player to bed, he slid under the covers and listened to Fin's deep voice talking dirty to him.

He reached down and stroked his hardened shaft. Fin's voice filled his head with images of the two of them. "Let me see you touch yourself, sweetheart. Ooh yeah, just like that. God, your cock is a thing of beauty." Mick stroked faster as Fin's voice went on. "Lick your finger…that's it…now spread those creamy cheeks and thrust inside that tight ass. Ooh…that's right, pump that ass."

Mick did as instructed, thrusting his hips, pushing and pulling as he shouted Fin's name and shot thick strings of semen onto his chest. He'd listened to the recording so many times he waited, knowing what came next. "Oh God, you're sexy. I love watching you come, sweetheart. Let me see you lick that hand clean. Oh yeah, just like that. I love you so much."

Mick smiled and left the recording on. He'd secretly taped Fin snoring and dubbed an hour of it onto the CD. Mick closed his eyes and fell asleep to the sound of his love snoring in his ears.

* * * * *

The next morning Fin couldn't get out of bed. He looked down at his bruised and swollen knee, thinking maybe he should just quit and give up the rest of the season but he was so close to finishing on a high note. He was wallowing in self-doubt when the phone beside the bed started ringing.

He smiled, Mick always called him after a game. He reached for the phone. "Good morning."

"Hey, baby. How are you feeling today?"

Fin tried to stretch out his sore knee. He winced with the pain. "Tired…a little sore. How 'bout you?"

He could hear Mick inhale deeply on the other end of the phone. "I'm fine. Worried about you. I know you don't wanna talk about it but I know about the knee. Evidently so does every team you play because they all go after it every chance they get."

Fin closed his eyes. "I didn't want you to know. Knew you'd be worried about me." He subconsciously ran his hand down his sore thigh to the swollen knee.

"How bad is it?"

He exhaled. "Bad. I can't even get outta bed this morning."

"I'll be there in a couple hours."

Mick didn't give him a chance to protest, he just hung up. Fin fell back onto the pillow. He knew he was taking a big chance letting Mick come, but damn, if he didn't need him. The season was almost over anyway so what the fuck. Now he just hoped Mick wouldn't try to talk him into not playing.

* * * * *

Mick had the manager call upstairs to get Fin's permission to unlock his door. He knew Fin would never make it across the apartment by himself. Opening the door for him, the manager gave Mick a nod and went back toward the elevator.

Mick set his bags down along with the fiddle. He'd taken it to a shop earlier in the week and had it restrung and tuned but he still couldn't bring himself to play it. He didn't plan on going home again until after the season when he could take Fin with him. He'd called the sound guys and musicians and told them they'd pick back up the second week in January.

He went to the bedroom and leaned against the doorframe. "Hey there, baby."

Fin held his hand out. "C'mere, I need you."

Walking over toward the bed, Mick stripped off his shirt and shoes. "Can I get you something for the pain?" He picked up the aspirin bottle off the table.

"I took three of those damn things but it's not helping."

"Don't you have anything stronger for the pain?" Mick couldn't believe he'd been trying to cope on just aspirin.

"The trainer gave me something but I haven't taken any. Pain's too constant. I don't wanna get addicted to the stuff."

Now that sounded more like his Fin. "Maybe just one to take the edge off. I won't let you become addicted."

Fin nodded once. "Just one then. They're in the medicine cabinet."

Mick retrieved the pill and filled the glass with fresh water. "You need to eat somethin' with this. Scrambled eggs sound okay to you?" He handed the pill and the glass of water to Fin.

"Thanks, sweetheart. Eggs are fine and maybe a cup of coffee if you don't mind."

Mick took the glass and set it back on the table. He bent over and kissed Fin. "Of course, I don't mind. I'm here to take care of you, dork." He headed out the bedroom door and turned his head. "Not leaving you alone. Gonna be here until the season's over and I take you home with me."

He returned a few minutes later with a bag in his hand. "What you're doing with a giant bag of frozen peas and nothing else but TV dinners in your freezer I don't know but it'll make a nice ice pack." He gently uncovered Fin's knee. "Fuck me. No wonder you can't stand on the son of a bitch."

Mick looked at the disfigured knee. "Fin, I think you need to go to the emergency room."

Shaking his head, Fin tried to sit up but the pain medicine was making him sleepy. "No, they'll make sure I don't play any more." He looked at Mick pleadingly. "I gotta play."

Mick looked from his face back to his knee. "Well, I guess I can always install a wheelchair ramp at the house." He turned on his heels and stormed back to the kitchen.

Making the eggs, Mick was still fuming. What the fuck was Fin thinking? He rubbed his forehead and tried to calm himself down. It was that damn promise he made to Sean. Mick looked toward the ceiling. "Do you see what he's doing for you, old man?"

He finished the eggs and put the plate on a little tray and took it into the bedroom. Fin was already asleep by the time he set the tray down beside him on the table. He hated to wake him up but puking up pain medicine wasn't going to do him any good either. He kissed Fin's cheek. "Wake up and eat a couple bites of these eggs."

Rubbing his eyes, Fin tried to sit up. "'M so sleepy."

"I know, but if you don't eat something you'll get sick." He went to the head of the bed and pushed Fin into a semi-sitting position and leaned him back against his chest. Taking a forkful of eggs, Mick fed him. Soon half the eggs on the plate were gone. "That's enough for now." He laid Fin back down on the pillow. "You sleep while I go to the grocery store and get some decent food into this place."

Fin mumbled something before he drifted off to sleep. Mick looked down on him as he picked up the egg plate. He really wanted to get in bed and snuggle with his Fin but knew he wouldn't be able to keep his hands off him, so he sighed and went to the store instead.

* * * * *

Three days later Fin still wasn't up to practicing with the team but he did manage to go in for the meetings. Mick found an old Chinese woman in Chinatown who sold him some herbal tea to help Fin with the pain and swelling.

He made sure Fin got a well-balanced meal every evening and massaged his knee every night. The team still had one away game left which was in three days. Fin would have to fly to Dallas on Saturday but then the final two games were at home in the Meadowlands.

When Fin got home that night he walked through the door and collapsed onto the couch. Mick went right over and sat down beside him. "Tough day?"

He nodded. "The trainers want me to sit this week's game out."

Mick ran his fingers through Fin's curls. "Maybe you should listen to them. If you miss this one game you'll surely be able to play the last two here at home." He kissed Fin's forehead. "Nothing to feel bad about. It's only one game."

"Yeah."

Mick knew that "little boy lost" face. He curled up against Fin and wrapped his arms around him. "We'll make you all better before next week, okay?"

Fin turned his head and kissed him deep. "Glad you're here." He rubbed Mick's stomach. "I wish I could fuck you. I miss that."

God, so did he. He got down on his knees in front of Fin and carefully spread his legs. "Just because you can't fuck doesn't mean I can't suck."

Fin smiled and spread his legs. Mick started on his zipper, lowering it down his erection. He opened the jeans and pulled down his underwear and Fin's beautiful cock sprang right out into his hands. "Not eager much, are you?"

Chuckling, Fin ran his fingers through Mick's hair. "Been a long time, sweetheart."

Running his tongue up the side of Fin's cock, Mick moaned. "Been hard to keep my hands off you." He swirled the weeping crown around in his mouth. He loved the way Fin tasted. He tongued the slit and got a thrust and a groan from Fin.

Smiling to himself, he took the entire length down his throat. Pulling off a little, he pumped his mouth up and down on the pulsing cock. He sucked and licked and occasionally even scraped with his teeth, driving Fin crazy.

"Need to come."

Pumping faster with his mouth, Mick reached down and rolled Fin's sac in his hand, squeezing gently. Fin thrust into his mouth and came. Mick could feel the heat as it slid down his throat to his stomach. He cleaned Fin up and stood in front of him.

Looking at Fin, he grinned. "My turn?" He started to unzip his jeans.

"Yes. Stand up here on the couch so I can reach you."

Fin helped him pull down his jeans and held his hand as he stood with one foot beside each of Fin's thighs. He still had to lean down a bit so Fin could reach his cock but better him moving and bending than Fin.

Fin started on his balls, licking and sucking his way around each one. Before moving up to his throbbing cock, he made a detour to his poor neglected hole. Mick put one foot up on the back of the couch to give Fin better access as his eyes rolled to the back of his head. "So good."

Fin's tongue rimmed his ass and snaked its way partially inside. He wet his finger and entered Mick's hole, searching for his pleasure gland. He hit it right away and Mick thrust his hips. "Oh Christ, yes."

Leaving his finger where it was, Fin licked his way back toward Mick's dripping cock. He used one hand to hold and rub and licked the tip. "Taste so good, sweetheart."

Mick thrust again and Fin gobbled him right up. The finger in Mick's ass continued its assault as Fin sucked and licked. Mick's stomach tightened as his head flew back. "Gonna come."

Fin thrust in another finger and Mick flooded his mouth with heat. Fin swallowed every drop and licked him clean. Collapsing beside Fin on the couch, Mick closed his eyes. "Oh fuck, I needed that."

* * * * *

Watching the game on television wasn't nearly as much fun as playing it but Fin did it anyway. The trainers had suggested he sit out the trip entirely and rest his knee. Fin thought the coaches just didn't want the press to see how bad his knee really was.

Mick tried to cheer him up the rest of the week but he just felt like he was breaking a promise. He knew it was dumb and that his da wouldn't have wanted him to play injured but he still felt like he was letting him down.

Mick sat down beside him with a huge plate of nachos. "You want some good game-day food?"

Bless him, he was really tryin'. "No thanks, sweetheart."

"Ya know the nachos in Jacksonville are way better than the ones in the Meadowland." He must have suddenly realized what he'd said because he looked down at his plate quickly.

Turning his head to look at Mick, Fin's eyebrow rose. "When did you have nachos in Jacksonville?"

Mick looked up a little sheepishly. "Last weekend when I went to see you play." Mick straightened and looked him in the eye, almost daring him to comment.

"You went to see one of my games? That's so cool but I wish you had told me." Fin rubbed Mick's thigh, smiling widely.

Mick cleared his throat. "Actually I've seen all but two games this year. I didn't wanna tell you because I thought it'd make you nervous."

Fin reached out and lifted Mick onto his lap. "Do you have any idea how much that means to me? I love that you did that. I love you."

Mick snuggled in. "I love you too, baby, and I love watching you play."

"Thanks, sweetheart. Just cross your fingers that I have two games left in this damn knee of mine."

Mick looked deep into his eyes. "You know that whether you play again or not you've fulfilled your promise." When Fin started to protest Mick held up his hand. "You promised Sean that you would dedicate this season to him. Right? Well, you've done that. It's all the newscasters talk about when discussing your success this season."

Fin nodded. "You're right. I've fulfilled my promise to Da but I need to finish this for me."

"Well then, it's a lucky thing you have me here to take care of you, huh?" Mick smiled, all smug and happy with himself.

"Yeah, it's a damn good thing I have you here." He stole a nacho off Mick's plate that had been carelessly dumped on the coffee table. "Let's finish watching the game in the bedroom. I think my knee's up to a little halftime entertainment." He waggled his eyebrows and grinned.

Mick shot off the couch like he was on fire. "Race ya. Last one there has to bring the beer."

"Hey, no way is that fair. I'm practically an invalid here." Fin stopped talking since Mick had left the room anyway. He shook his head and chuckled, heading for the kitchen.

* * * * *

Mick was so excited he was bouncing. Today was the last game of the season and the last game of Fin's career. Fin didn't know it but the team was planning a little celebration after the game on the field. Mick had gone to the team owners and asked special permission to perform the Irish ballad "On the Banks of Lee" for Fin at the end of the celebration. He'd explained to the owners that he was Ian Gallagher and both Sean's and Fin's favorite singer.

Of course he didn't tell them that he was Fin's lover and the song he was going to perform was kinda like "their song" but what they didn't know wouldn't hurt them. They even gave Mick special permission to sit up in the broadcast booth to watch the game.

It had been hell keeping the secret all week from Fin but he thought he'd done a pretty good job of it. Now as he sat behind the wall of glass looking down at the field he felt an immense sense of relief. If Fin could just make it through this game his promise to himself and his da would be fulfilled.

At the end of the first quarter Fin rushed for a touchdown, making him one short of breaking his record. Mick could overhear the sports announcers talking about Fin's unbelievable season and the little tidbit about him dedicating it to his deceased father. They went on to discuss his retirement from football and what a shock it was to the entire football community.

Fin had gone on record the previous week about his plans to retire a year early but refused to give the press a reason. He simply stated that it was time. Mick smiled, remembering the celebration the two of them had enjoyed after the press conference.

They'd talked a lot in the past week about what they were going to do with the rest of their lives. They even discussed returning to run the pub. The city had passed a nonsmoking ordinance that went into effect in January. Mick knew that some of the pub patrons wouldn't be happy about the nonsmoking ordinance but Fin was ecstatic. They decided in the end to take it easy for another couple years so Mick could finish recording the CDs he wanted to do and they still planned on touring some of the regional pubs.

At halftime they announced the plans for the retirement celebration after the end of the game to the fans in the stadium. Mick wished he could see Fin's face right about now. With the smile still on his face his cell phone began vibrating. Puzzled, he picked it up and looked at the caller ID. The call was coming from somewhere inside the stadium. "Hello?"

"Did you know about this celebration they have planned?"

Mick chuckled. "Told you I could keep a secret."

"I can't believe they're doin' it. I mean, I'm just a regular player. Those celebrations are usually reserved for the Hall of Fame guys."

Oh, his Fin was still so modest, never believing he was good enough. "You will be one of those Hall of Fame guys, baby." He caught what he'd said and looked around to make sure no one was listening to him.

"Oh, I don't know about that but it still feels great to know I matter to the team that much."

Mick could hear the coach yelling in the background. "Gotta go, sweetheart. I'm fixin' to get an ass chewing for being on the phone. Love ya."

"Love you."

* * * * *

With under three minutes left in the game it didn't look like New York was going to win. They were down by twenty-one points and Fin was really moving slowly. Mick caught him limping off the field several times. A loss wouldn't make the celebration quite the same but Fin had given his all today, he just didn't have the backup he needed to get the job done.

Fin ran down the edge of the field and leapt in the air to catch a thirty-five-yard pass. As he was coming back down one of the Redskins tackled him from the left side, driving his helmet into Fin's left knee. Fin crumpled to the field and held his sore knee.

The fans in the stadium were outraged and they let the Redskins know it. Mick could hear the sports announcers talking about cheap shots and career-ending injuries. The side judge ruled out of bounds and the crowd once again erupted in boos and hisses against the decision. Mick stood and pressed his hands to the glass as the team physician and coaches gathered around Fin.

Mick held his breath. His poor Fin only had another two minutes left to play in his career, with only eight yards needed for a record-breaking touchdown and now Mick was afraid he'd be taken off the field on a stretcher. Not the way Fin wanted it to end. He looked around the press box, trying to figure out what he could do to help. The fans outside in the stadium were about to tear the place apart in outrage and something needed to be done.

The stadium announcer tried to calm the crowd by informing them the officials were watching the replays to determine where Fin's feet were when he was tackled to the ground. Nothing the announcer said seemed enough for the bloodthirsty crowd.

Mick closed his eyes and said a quick prayer to his mother and Sean and picked up his fiddle case off the floor. He opened the case and took out the fiddle. It felt so natural in his hands he couldn't believe it'd been over six years since he'd played it. He walked to the stadium announcer's booth and spoke to him in a hushed voice. The announcer shrugged his shoulders and stepped back. At this point nothing could make the crowd any worse than they already were.

Mick stepped up to the microphone and swallowed around the lump in his throat. He was afraid he might throw up before he got through this. With the crowd going crazy outside Mick placed the fiddle under his chin and began to play "Danny Boy". Both Mick and Fin knew it was Sean's all-time favorite Irish ballad.

As he played the crowd began to look around them and look up at the booth. No doubt wondering what the hell was going on. To Mick's knowledge this was the first time anyone dared to play a fiddle in the announcers' booth over the stadium loudspeakers.

It began working and the crowd quieted down and all eyes fixed on Fin still lying on the field. Once the crowd quieted down Fin must have been able to hear the fiddle because he managed to sit up and look around him. Mick could see him talking to the coach and then the coach pointed up to the booth.

Fin looked up and Mick could swear their eyes met. Mick poured his heart and soul into the song. When the song ended the crowd went wild. Mick smiled and decided to play one more song just for Fin. "On the Banks of Lee" sounded through the stadium speakers and it seemed that was just what Fin needed to hear because he started arguing with the physician and the coaches to stand him up.

They got Fin on his feet but it was obvious that he couldn't stand on his own. Mick knew he wouldn't be able to finish the game. The crowd however didn't agree and as they took Fin to the sidelines to resume the game the crowd started chanting Fin's name.

The head referee came out onto the field and informed the screaming fans that after further reviewing the replay Fin's feet had been inbounds at the time of the tackle. New York would retain possession of the ball on the eight-yard line.

Although the fans were happy about the call, they wanted Fin back out on the field. They began chanting his name again.

The noise in the stadium was so deafening that the Redskins called a timeout. The coach motioned his defensive captain to the sidelines. The captain talked to the coach and nodded his head. The captain ran back onto the field and talked to New York's quarterback.

Mick was standing beside the stadium announcer as he tried to make sense of what was going on down on the field. The quarterback signaled another timeout, this time for the offense and ran to the sidelines to talk to his coach. As the entire stadium went quiet, Fin limped, with the help of the quarterback, onto the field.

The entire stadium chanted, "Fin…ne…gan, Fin…ne…gan," over and over. Mick could feel the love in the stadium on both sides. As he watched, the quarterback took the snap and ran the ball to Fin. Fin accepted the ball and with a nod to the Redskins defense he began to limp toward the end zone. The Redskins stood and applauded as Fin got closer to the record-breaking touchdown.

The announcer in the booth was going nuts, yelling and chanting Fin's name along with the crowd. Fin managed to cross the goal line just as the game-ending buzzer sounded. Fin fell once again but this time Mick had a feeling it was more from emotion than pain. His entire team ran to the end zone to help him celebrate.

Carrying Fin on their shoulders, the team gathered in the center of the field. The Redskins all came out to the center and Fin shook each and every player's hand.

Mick didn't even realize he was crying until the announcer handed him a box of tissues and smiled. "Why don't you go on down there, son? I'll make sure they clear a path for you." The older man picked up a phone and a security guard appeared in the doorway.

He ushered Mick down onto the field. Mick refused the offer to go to the fifty-yard line with Fin. This was Fin's moment to shine. He didn't need to share it with a blubbering fool.

After Fin shook the last hand, the New York team carried him off the field to the sideline. They put Fin down on the team bench. Mick could see the emotions begin to overwhelm Fin and he longed to go to him. Mick slowly walked toward the bench with the security guard right behind him.

Fin was shaking a few more hands when he looked up and spotted Mick. He somehow managed to stand and held out his hand to him. Mick's eyes widened but he took Fin's hand. "You did it. You finished the season and kept your promise."

Fin squeezed Mick's hand. "I'm more proud of you for playin' that fiddle than I am of myself right now. It was beautiful. I could've never asked for a better ending to my career than to hear that fiddle playing over the speakers."

Mick shrugged his shoulders and leaned in to talk into Fin's ear. "I guess we both worked through our grief this season. Now we can think about our future instead of our past."

Fin grinned and licked his ear. He didn't care who knew Mick was the love of his life. He'd fulfilled all his promises to both the fans and his da. Now it was his turn to live the life he wanted. "Past or future, it doesn't matter as long as we're in it together."

Also by Carol Lynne

ℰᴑ

eBooks:

Feels So Right

Finnegan's Promise

Gio's Dream

Harvest Heat

Men in Love 1: Branded by Gold

Men in Love 2: Ben's Wildflower

Men in Love 3: Open to Possibilities

Men in Love 4: Completing the Circle

Men in Love 5: Going Against Orders

Men in Love 6: Tortured Souls

Necklace of Shame

Never Too Old

No Longer His

Riding the Wolf

Saddle Up and Ride 1: Reining in the Past

Saddle Up and Ride 2: Bareback Cowboy

Sex With Lex

Sunshine, Sex and Sunflowers

Print Books:

Down Under Temptation *(anthology)*

Forbidden Love *(anthology)*

Men in Love 1 & 2: Branded by Love

Men in Love 3: Open to Possibilities

Men in Love 4: Completing the Circle
Naughtiest Nuptials *(anthology)*
Protected Love *(anthology)*
Taboo Treats *(anthology)*

About the Author

ॐ

I've been a reading fanatic for years and finally at the age of 40 decided to try my hand at writing. I've always loved romance novels that are just a little bit naughty so naturally my books tend to go just a little further. It's my fantasy world after all.

When I'm not being a mother to a five-year-old and a six-year-old, you can usually find me in my deep leather chair with either a book in my hand or my laptop.

ॐ

The author welcomes comments from readers. You can find her website and email address on her author bio page at www.ellorascave.com.

Tell Us What You Think

We appreciate hearing reader opinions about our books. You can email us at Comments@EllorasCave.com.

Why an electronic book?

We live in the Information Age—an exciting time in the history of human civilization, in which technology rules supreme and continues to progress in leaps and bounds every minute of every day. For a multitude of reasons, more and more avid literary fans are opting to purchase e-books instead of paper books. The question from those not yet initiated into the world of electronic reading is simply: *Why?*

1. ***Price.*** An electronic title at Ellora's Cave Publishing runs anywhere from 40% to 75% less than the cover price of the exact same title in paperback format. Why? Basic mathematics and cost. It is less expensive to publish an e-book (no paper and printing, no warehousing and shipping) than it is to publish a paperback, so the savings are passed along to the consumer.

2. ***Space.*** Running out of room in your house for your books? That is one worry you will never have with electronic books. For a low one-time cost, you can purchase a handheld device specifically designed for e-reading. Many e-readers have large, convenient screens for viewing. Better yet, hundreds of titles can be stored within your new library—on a single microchip. There are a variety of e-readers from different manufacturers. You can also read e-books on your PC or laptop computer. (Please note that Ellora's Cave does not endorse any specific brands.

You can check our website at www.ellorascave.com for information we make available to new consumers.)

3. *Mobility.* Because your new e-library consists of only a microchip within a small, easily transportable e-reader, your entire cache of books can be taken with you wherever you go.

4. *Personal Viewing Preferences.* Are the words you are currently reading too small? Too large? Too… ANNOYING? Paperback books cannot be modified according to personal preferences, but e-books can.

5. *Instant Gratification.* Is it the middle of the night and all the bookstores near you are closed? Are you tired of waiting days, sometimes weeks, for bookstores to ship the novels you bought? Ellora's Cave Publishing sells instantaneous downloads twenty-four hours a day, seven days a week, every day of the year. Our webstore is never closed. Our e-book delivery system is 100% automated, meaning your order is filled as soon as you pay for it.

Those are a few of the top reasons why electronic books are replacing paperbacks for many avid readers.

As always, Ellora's Cave welcomes your questions and comments. We invite you to email us at Comments@ellorascave.com or write to us directly at Ellora's Cave Publishing Inc., 1056 Home Avenue, Akron, OH 44310-3502.

ELLORA'S CAVE

Romanticon

Annual convention
for women who
refuse to behave

Discover for yourself why readers can't get enough
of the multiple award-winning publisher
Ellora's Cave.

Whether you prefer e-books or paperbacks,

be sure to visit EC on the web at
www.ellorascave.com

for an erotic reading experience that will leave you
breathless.

Lightning Source UK Ltd.
Milton Keynes UK
UKOW051700270712

196686UK00001B/98/P